Y0-EFV-681

THE FURYS
OF
CAPISTRANO

THE FURYS
OF
CAPISTRANO

•

Jeanette Sparks

AVALON BOOKS
NEW YORK

PRINTED IN THE UNITED STATES OF AMERICA
ON ACID-FREE PAPER
BY HADDON CRAFTSMEN, BLOOMSBURG, PENNSYLVANIA

This book is dedicated to my dear sister Colleen, my role model, who has always been there to spur me on to accomplish my goals.

Chapter One

Erin Fury dropped the letter on the scarred desktop, its message burning her fingertips like a hot skillet. The more she thought about the demand to vacate the ranch in ninety days, the angrier she grew. Their new landlord, Regency College, had sprouted up two years ago just outside the ranch. They couldn't do this to her family—not after the Furys had lived nearly twenty years on this small horse ranch. She'd fight any idea the board of trustees had to flatten the land in the name of progress.

"Where will we go?" her father, Mike, asked. Shocked, his arms hung limp at his sides, as he watched her pace across the plank floor of their tiny, rustic office in the stables.

Erin stopped and looked over her shoulder at his

leathery face and smiled with deep affection. She wished he could find a good, loving woman to fill his loneliness. Her mother had died the year before. "We're not going anywhere, Dad. Sit tight. I'll be back soon, after I've had a nose-to-nose talk with that new college president. That man's trying to make a name for himself at our expense."

His face went slack and he slumped into a chair, holding his head in his calloused palms. "So it has come to this. The world is rushing in right behind us. I'm afraid this is a wake-up call to some harsh realities."

Erin stormed out of the office, past the curious horses in their stalls, and jumped into her dusty red Jeep Cherokee, slamming the door. The engine roared and she took off down the country lane that led to the exclusive private college bordering their ranch. Blood boiling, she drove like a madwoman, while keeping one eye peeled on the rearview mirror for the patrol.

She didn't slow down until she reached the entrance gates and turned into a visitor's slot in front of the administration building. The towering walls of academia stood out imposingly bright in the noonday sun as her boots tapped a cadence on the cement steps.

Glancing down at her work clothes, blue jeans and laced-up boots, she asked herself why she hadn't taken time to change. Instead, she was charging in there like an angry bull. Too late now for niceties. The illustrious president probably patted his cheeks with great smelling Polo after shaving, whereas she must smell like sweaty horsehair and dirt.

Two students holding identical notebooks, lounged

against a wall, flirting with one another. The pretty young woman had a butterfly tattoo on her neck and the male student had shaved his head. What was college coming to? She'd only left Cal. State Fullerton six years ago—and now this?

Inside the building, Erin glanced around until she found a roster listing the offices. She hurried down the central hall to the Office of the President, took a deep breath, and barged in. A middle-aged woman, neatly dressed with a narrow nose and tired eyes, insisted Erin couldn't see the top man.

"Mr. Archer is tied up on a conference call. You'll need to make an appointment, dear," the secretary said from behind the metal desk, her voice slightly condescending.

Erin wasn't about to take no for an answer. "Archer sent me a letter. I demand to see him right away or I'll sit here in this office until I do."

"Well, if you must." The woman zipped her lips, ready for the standoff.

Twenty minutes passed while Erin, agitated, thumbed through a college brochure and several magazines without reading them.

She stood up and stared at her wristwatch, then at the woman, tapping her foot. "Mr. Archer's conference call must be over with by now. Tell him Erin Fury is here to see him. And I don't have all day."

The secretary cleared her throat. "I can't interrupt him. He's attending to other important business just now."

Erin placed her hands on the desk and leaned forward. "Listen! My time is important, too. I've got a bunch of disabled kids coming over for riding lessons. You tell him I want to see him pronto or I will."

The woman, her mouth set in a thin line of disapproval, rose, unhurried, and strode to the president's private office. She knocked softly, then entered. Moments later, she returned, leaving the door ajar. "Mr. Archer will see you now, Mrs. Fury."

"Miss Fury," Erin said, and glided past her. "Thanks."

An awkward moment followed when the secretary introduced Erin to Jordan Archer in his stylish inner sanctum. Then she closed the door behind her. Erin had to tip her head back to look at him. She was expecting someone with thinning hair and a spare tire. This man, tall and intensely physical, was nothing like that. If she hadn't been so angry, she'd probably have been very impressed.

Archer remained standing, a slightly annoyed expression on his face. He wasn't much over thirty, Erin noted. A bleached mahogany desk divided them. Framed certificates and diplomas hung on the walls, along with a fine painting of the jewel of the old California missions in San Juan Capistrano. Shelves of important looking books and matching leather chairs spoke volumes about the consumption of wealth.

Archer took a good look at Erin, from the crown of her head, to the smudges on her well-worn boots. His annoyance turned to amusement as his slate-gray eyes flickered. It wasn't lost on her. Most likely he didn't touch the ground when he walked like ordinary men, she thought contemptuously. And he probably never had a hard time finding a parking place, either.

"Won't you sit down?" He extended his tanned hand to one of the leather chairs.

"No, thank you. This won't take long," she said, direct and to the point. "My father and I run the stables next to the college. This morning we received a letter saying our lease won't be renewed. What's this all about?"

Anger pumped adrenaline through her veins as the dark-haired man listened, his squarish face now expressionless. His pin-striped, three-pieced suit, wing-tipped shoes and salon trimmed hair pegged him as a wimp in her book. He probably never let anyone catch him without creases in his trousers. The thought brought her close to a nervous chuckle. But she had to admit, though with disdain, he wasn't bad looking.

Jordan Archer tried not to let his gaze stay too long on her. Erin Fury was a small woman, with a slight, graceful figure and fair complexion hidden under a tan. She filled out the faded jeans in an eye-catching way. He forced his attention back to her oval face in time to read the frustration simmering there. Her hazel eyes peered at him like hard, glittering stones. How old was she—maybe mid-twenties? A mass of wild russet hair framed her pretty face. The downward curve of her mouth could only spell trouble. Then he remembered why she was here. Something about the lease.

"I'm afraid it's absolutely necessary," he said, sitting down. "The college bought the land recently, as you are aware. We're growing, and we need those twenty acres for new dorms and an extended parking lot."

Her shoulders thrust back. "You can't pave over

everything. Please reconsider before it's too late. Don't you understand we're important to this community? Not only do we board and rescue horses, we also work with handicapped children, teaching them to horseback ride. It gives them a sense of freedom and accomplishment. Why, we even board some of your students' horses and they come over on weekends to volunteer."

He measured his words. "Sounds commendable, but surely you won't have a problem relocating elsewhere in the valley."

She took the suggestion with all the enthusiasm of a Kabuki actor, solemn face and all. Yet Jordan had to hand it to her, she sounded intelligent and resolute— a go-get'em kind of gal.

"Don't you realize we haven't any other place that's suitable," she said. Her voice was tough and articulate with a sweet bravado. "Land is at a premium in this county. You simply can't do this." Her jaw set stubbornly.

He tried to keep control of the situation but Erin Fury hurried on, dominating the conversation. She reminded him in no uncertain terms of how long the Furys had lived on the ranch.

"Maybe you aren't aware," she said, "but twenty years of our lives have been poured into making that place what it is today. Just what are we supposed to do, turn those horses over to a glue factory and break the kids' hearts?"

He could see this woman's determination to steamroll this issue to victory and he hated to refuse her, yet he had his own priorities. She might be smart and savvy, but she had an attitude that irritated him. Butting heads with her wasn't going to be fun.

"Sorry, but that's the way things are," he said. "The board of trustees came to an agreement on the property's use at their last month's meeting."

"Nothing's written in concrete," she fired back.

Jordan sighed ruefully. Erin Fury was a feisty tomboy who probably kickboxed for a hobby. So why did he want to console her? He couldn't prevent himself from feeling a certain compassion and sympathy for her cause. Those big, expressive eyes, almost too big for her small face, vacillated between anger and sadness—and somehow enchanted him.

Erin held his gaze, then exhaled in utter frustration when he looked away.

This turkey's insane if he thinks I'll give up easily, she told herself, biting her lower lip.

Archer glanced at his watch just as the telephone rang. He picked up the receiver and talked with his back to her. She tried not to listen as she composed her next argument. However, when he raised his voice, she went on instant alert. *Something about a proposed burgeoning enrollment next semester*. Well, that was just too darn bad. This ritzy college could build its dorms somewhere else.

When he hung up, he turned back to Erin, rested his strong fingers on the edge of the desk, and spoke with a studied countenance. "You were saying?"

Erin had a furious urge to pace, a characteristic inherited from her father, but forced down the impulse. Okay, she'd play Mr. Cool's game.

Mustering a calmer demeanor, she flubbed her next words. "Mr. Coo . . . uh . . . I mean Archer, you simply can't do this. We need that land more than the college does. The ranch means everything to those kids, as well as to us."

His fleeting half-life of interest seemed to dwindle when the phone rang again. Erin fumed, shifting her stance. He scribbled something on a message pad. The man was too darned taken with his own self-importance. He must think her a mere peasant and himself king of the hill. He'd probably be surprised to know she'd gone to college, too, even if she did drop out before graduating to help on the ranch.

When he replaced the receiver, Archer said, "Sorry to keep you waiting. Busy day. Now where were we? Ah—the ranch. The board's made its decision. I don't see them changing direction now."

"And you have no say in the matter? Couldn't you explain about the circumstances—the service we perform for the community?"

"Well, maybe . . ."

"So, go tell them we need to keep that land."

"Now Mrs. Fury, it isn't that easy."

Her lips parted. "It's Miss."

"I stand corrected. The determination, as I said before, was made weeks ago. We're presently in negotiations with an architectural firm."

She leaned over the desk, far into his space. "Cancel it!"

Somehow he knew this woman was going to be more then a blip on a radar screen. He saw the college's plan as a necessary expansion, even if she saw it as a doomsday scenario.

"I can't help you," he said, rising, "and I'm late for a meeting."

"With the board? I'll go along and spell out our position."

"No," he mused dryly. "My meeting's not with the board." He grabbed his expensive leather attaché case off a low file cabinet. "I apologize for cutting this short but I must go now."

She hedged, and parked her bottom on the corner of his desk. "Okay, I'll take only one more minute of your time. Back to square one. I don't understand what you're saying. Could you explain all this to me again? Dorm rooms for a projected enrollment are more important than handicapped kids and mistreated horses—right?"

He'd reached halfway across the room when he stopped and turned back. This time he didn't mince words. "The answer is still an unequivocal no."

She jumped down. "You could have said no in less words. What a cop-out! You don't care squat what happens to us." It was a statement, not a question. "Well, you haven't heard the last from me. We'll hire an attorney. Jerry Spence would just love to take on a case like this."

He looked tired. "Really? Hire him then. But it won't make any difference. Legally, the property belongs to the college and everything on it. Now, good day, Miss Fury."

The bluff didn't work; and his flat refusal stunned Erin. Her palms started sweating. This interchange was one of the lowest points in her life. She spun on her heel and stomped out of his office ahead of him.

When Erin arrived home, she parked behind the barn to lick her wounds in private. Sitting in the Cherokee under an expansive cedar tree, she stared at the old building's chipped paint and the broken-down windmill to its side. The spindly wheel barely moved in the growing breeze. Rain was forecasted. A horse whinnied in the pasture. The familiar sound comforted her briefly but the thought of losing the place caused an unbearable sadness to wash over her in despairing waves.

Erin loved her life. The only thing missing was the right man. She wanted romance, love, and marriage, but she had been too busy to do much about it.

With an abysmal sigh, she opened the car door and headed back to the office in the stables. Fresh feed filled the stall mangers, and the automatic water feeders they'd recently installed at great expense kept the water crystal clear. She strode past the tack room and peered at the neat rows of saddles and gear. No one else was around, although volunteers would arrive within the hour to help with the disabled children.

She found Archer's letter where she'd tossed it on the desktop. Reading the cold words once again caused her stomach muscles to knot with dread. So the college planned to run them off the land? Some power deep inside her rose up and she seethed, "Over my dead body!"

Erin opened a squeaky desk drawer and threw the envelope in, closing it with a bang. She took a seat in the old captain's chair and tackled a stack of papers, but her heart wasn't in it. Finally, she gave up. How could anyone concentrate after what she'd been through? She leaned back in the chair, placed her booted feet on the desk, cupped her hands behind her neck, and tried to think of a way out of this appalling dilemma.

Her father lumbered through the open door, a frown on his face. A big man, his features were chiseled like granite from years in the sun. The bad news threatened everything he held dear. His eyes glinted with suppressed rage. Seeing him so unhappy made her want to cry. Her mother's death had been an awful blow to him, and now this had to happen.

"Hi, Dad," Erin said, fighting to hold her voice steady.

"Met with them, did you now?"

She pulled her feet down from the desk. "Yeah."

"And?" His tone rose. "Spill it out, girl. Just what's going on? You should have taken me with you."

"It's real bad. The new college president wouldn't give an inch. They're set on turning this place into a concrete jungle."

His fists clenched. "This can't be happening to us. It just can't."

He paced the floor, his scuffed boots grating on the wood.

"C'mon, Dad, sit down. We'll think of something."

He finally slumped into a chair across from his daughter. Taking out bifocals, he perched them on the tip of his nose and asked to see the letter again. She took the envelope out of the drawer and handed it to him.

He scanned the contents, then slammed the letter down. "They're a bunch of mules!"

Erin nodded. "Make it jackasses."

Her father hooked an arm over the back of the chair.

"What next? We ought to take action immediately and . . ." His voice trailed away.

Erin watched his eyes compress and she worried about his blood pressure rising. "We won't take this lying down. There are other avenues."

He gave her a grim nod. A moment of silent understanding passed between them. Outside, inclement weather rolled in off the ocean. She glanced through the windowpane. Steel-wool clouds darkened the sky, then let loose a barrage of turbulent fat drops. The air thickened with wind and rain, rattling window casings, and pummeled the roof like something out of a bad dream.

Erin switched on a light. "It's late in the season for a rain storm."

"Yeah, almost time for the swallows to arrive for the big festival."

She stared into space, unable to focus on anything for very long. "Some people declare fighting city hall is a pipe dream. They'd say it's not practical—just forget the whole miserable thing. But that's not the way we're made, Dad, you and me."

"Absolutely not," he replied, perking up a tad. "We Furys are fighters. Goes back to our Irish ancestors. I remember tales of your grandpa fighting for the cause over there."

"It's going to be tough, but in my heart I have faith we'll overcome this obstacle. We'll just keep on trying 'til we do. Let them build those blasted dorms in another location."

"Right!"

"But it's risky."

"What's risky? They already want us out," he

growled, splitting the air with his hairy fist. "After all these years, I can't comprehend their reasoning. Like a bust in the chops, it is."

Erin didn't like the resigned look in his eyes, even if his words and body language said something quite different. Ever since her mother's death, he didn't have much fight left in him. She knew how much he missed his life's helpmate. It didn't seem fair the way fate had separated them.

His once coal black hair had hints of silver and the lines on his face showed the telltale signs of aging. Although he had a gruff exterior, it couldn't hide his heart of gold. Just the day before when he finished helping a mare deliver a foal, he'd wept at the beauty of birth. Erin loved and respected him with all her being, and it hurt to see his drooping shoulders.

"We'll hire an attorney," she said.

He shook his head. "You know we don't have money for one of those fellas, darlin'. It would take a barrel of greenbacks."

In frustration, she pushed the chair back. "I know it, but we won't give up until they cart us off the ranch, kicking and screaming."

Her mouth was dry and she got up and opened a bottle of spring water from the small refrigerator in the corner of the room. "What one?" He shook his head. After taking a healthy gulp, she said, "We can go before the city council. They're usually not pro growth. Remember how they stood up to all those fast food corporations? Maybe we could get them to deny the college's building permit."

He grinned. "That's my lass. Always the brainy one. You're the light of my life. Maybe I should have been a banker, or judge, or something important so I could provide for you better."

She held his hands and glanced down at the callouses. "You are important. The most important man in the world."

Her father's mouth relaxed.

That night in bed, Erin wept as she hadn't since her mother's death. When the floodgates dribbled to an end, she grabbed another tissue out of the box beside the bed and blew her nose. She stared soberly up at the dusky shadows on the ceiling. Sleep wouldn't come easily. Far away in the distance a train whistle interrupted the night's calm.

Hours later, in restless sleep, Erin flailed around the bed, wadding the sheets as an army of medieval soldiers in black body armor chased her through a forest of barren trees. Thorny branches reached out to slow her escape. Heart racing, she reached the edge of a cliff. Just as she was about to hurl over to the ocean below, she came out of the mist. Lucky, her yellow Labrador, licked her face, saving her from imminent disaster.

Erin struggled to sit up and blinked her eyes, then ruffled the Lab's ears.

"What a noble dog you are!" she said.

During breakfast that morning, Erin racked her brain for a solution to their predicament. Unable to eat, she placed her cereal bowl on the floor for Lucky to lap up.

"Dad, let me see the original lease," she said.

"I think it's in the old file." He sat at the kitchen table, making an X with his spoon in the bowl.

"The one you hauled out to the barn? That's no place to keep important papers."

He looked nonplused. "What do you want with it?"

"Just curious. It won't hurt to take a glance at the original wording."

"Mrs. Fielding was a nice old lady. Not like her son, Denny, who couldn't wait to unload this property. Wanted to start living the high life as soon as she was in the ground." He ran his fingers through his bushy hair. "I'll dig out the lease, if the mice haven't already eaten the paper. But I'm afraid it won't do any good at this point."

He hung his head and stared stonily at his hat hanging on a nail by the door but he didn't get up. Erin came around the table, giving him a hug, fearful of what this would do to him. "Don't worry, Dad, we'll think of something." She took a deep, tremulous breath. *And pigs fly.*

Much too soon, their bucolic life would catapult to an immediate close. What could they possibly do to change the outcome?

Chapter Two

Ten days later Erin learned the city council turned down their request to have the dormitory building plans rescinded. Things couldn't have looked bleaker. The ninety days seemed to be slipping away like grains of sand in her palm.

Erin went from high spirits to the doldrums. Everything had changed. Why hadn't they foreseen the black cloud on the horizon? She and her father always assumed the lease would be renewed without a hitch— a mere formality. But they should have known better. Mrs. Fielding's son never cherished the land with the intensity of his mother.

Erin tapped her foot under the table. This was all Archer's fault! Why couldn't he leave things the way they had been? She'd like to see him drawn and quartered. But what could she expect from a donkeyish man like him.

"It's a blue Monday for us, girl," her father said, twisting his lips.

Erin nodded. She stared down at her wobbly poached egg. For some reason it looked as though it was smiling up at her like a one-eyed monster from another galaxy. She had no appetite and pushed it away.

"Dad, to get the trustees to delay this thing is about the best we can hope for. If we can convince them to do that, maybe something else will materialize."

"What a rotten thing they did to us, wanting to destroy my life's work this way," he snapped.

She grimaced. "I find Jordan Archer arrogant and just a tad above Vlad—The Impaler. I'm sure he's the one who instigated this whole thing."

Mike didn't respond to her glib remark. He opened his mouth and made a cavernous yawn. "In a dream last night I saw bulldozers rolling across our property. They pulled down the barn, the stables and followed with the house. A pitiful sight it was to see. Then they ate the orange grove, one beautiful old tree at a time." His eyes clouded. "This peaceful patch of land mustn't vanish like so many others here in the valley, hon."

"I'll go over to the college today and make our proposal, clean and neat. We need another year. By then, we'll have found something else. Surely Archer will listen to reason." But secretly she held out little hope.

"Don't get bogged down in haggling the nitty-gritty. Let them raise the rent. Anything. We'll manage somehow. Better still, lemme talk to that stuffy big-shot," he said, his voice deepening. "I'll tell him a thing or two."

"You're needed here, Dad. The Smiths are bringing in the gelding they found trotting along the Ortega Highway."

"Always things needing to be done around here," he fussed. "No one out looking for the horse as yet?"

"No calls so far."

She gave her dish to the dog, then rinsed it at the sink.

"Josh and his mom should be pulling in about now," she said, confirming with a quick glance through the window. "I better get out there."

Sarah Whitefeather was already helping her disabled son down from the battered panel truck when Erin walked through the door. Rocky, the black and white tomcat, stood on the sidelines, meowing. She bent down and stroked the full arch of his spine.

"Fine day for a ride," Sarah said.

"Just great." Erin sauntered over to them and slicked back the boy's cowlick with her palm. "You ready for a ride, tiger?"

The ten-year-old, dark-haired boy, gave her a bright-eyed, confident smile. "Sure am, Erin."

Sarah tossed her son a maternal smile. "Don't forget your helmet."

A colt looked up curiously from under an august oak tree in the pasture and nickered softly. Another horse lifted its head and snorted. Josh chuckled, calling to them by name.

"I've got Ol' Paint saddled and ready to go," Erin said.

They strolled to the hitching post in front of the

stables, making allowances for Josh's slower speed. The pony, patiently waiting, twisted his neck to eye the boy. Erin helped Josh mount. Josh smacked a wad of gum between his jaws as he sat astride the horse, holding the reins in his tight fists. Erin took a short lead rope and led the horse into the arena, dreading the thought of breaking the bad news to Josh and his mother.

The boy had gained faith in his ability, but she could tell by the stiffness of his shoulders that he remained a bit nervous. "Try to turn your knees in a little, Josh," she directed. "That's good. Hold the reins firmly but not too tight. There. Uh-huh. Don't be frightened. I'm right here."

"I'm not afraid anymore," he said with a touch of pride.

"That's my boy," Sarah called out from where she reclined against a fence post. "You're going to be a knock-'em-dead cowboy."

Josh grinned. He suffered from muscular dystrophy and his muscles were weak. He was one of forty disabled children brought to the ranch each week for lessons. His mother Sarah, a devoted single parent, was Erin's close friend. They had known each other since high school.

Erin focused on Josh's posture in the saddle. She loved the boy. Deliberate in his task, Josh took to the challenge. He posed in the saddle like a child who had no problems. Sitting astride the calm pony, he let his smile tumble over her like a welcoming spray of spring blossoms.

"Oh!" he cried. "Something bit me."

"Where?" She glanced around for a bumblebee.

"Right here." He pointed to his forearm.

Erin looked but didn't notice any signs. "I don't see anything. It must be your imagination."

"Does imaginations bite cha'?" he asked, wide-eyed.

She couldn't control the chuckle that bubbled up. Sarah laughed too, and finally the boy, realizing it was only a gnat bite.

The lesson went well. Josh didn't need to use a special saddle anymore. When it was over, Erin helped him dismount, heartsick about having to tell them the bad news.

She tethered the horse to a hitching post. "I'll walk you to the truck."

"I sure had a good time," Josh said. He took off his helmet and squinted.

"Good. That's what riding is all about."

"Can I ride the new thoroughbred sometime?"

"Maybe, if he ever gets gentled."

Sarah winked at Erin as she slid back the truck door. Her boy always wanted to do things he couldn't.

Erin steeled herself to tell them the bad news, not holding anything back.

"Regency College bought our property and they've told us they don't intend to renew the lease. In simple words, we're being forced out."

The looks on their faces was a real kick in the stomach. Sarah, usually upbeat, looked crestfallen.

"No!" she cried.

"I don't know how to make this tragic news any easier for everyone," Erin said with anguish.

Sarah swore under her breath. "Surely they will reconsider. What can they be thinking? You've been running this successful, nonprofit program for close to ten years. Josh could hardly wait until he was old enough to sign up. His doctor says he's made great strides, partly because of this opportunity."

Erin shook her head. "The board's giving in is about as remote as Saddam Hussein being given honorary U.S. citizenship," she said with a bitterness in her voice she didn't try to hide.

"This is going to send shock waves through the community," Sarah said.

"I know. This land has been a working ranch for as far back as most old-timers can remember."

"You've got to fight them."

"We intend to do just that," she replied, her voice quavering.

Josh wrinkled his mouth in disappointment. Erin's sympathy went out to him. She took his hand and wrapped it in both of hers. "We'll do our best to stay here, Josh. You haven't seen the last of us yet."

He gave her a brave smile but his voice trembled. "I hope so, Erin. I'd sure miss Ol' Paint."

She had to fight to keep hers steady. "We won't let you down."

Sarah glanced around. "There's something about this ranch that breaks my heart in two when I think of your losing it. But having the property flattened and cemented over has to be the very worst. Progress! Boo!"

The blood drummed in Erin's temples. "We're forced to confront a reality we had long chosen to ignore." She sighed heavily. "We have a real skirmish on our hands, Sarah. If you can think of something, let me know."

*   *   *

Situated in a far corner of the ranch surrounded by cedar trees and a garden, the Fury's turn-of-the-century house blended with the coffee-colored terrain. A historic landmark, it would probably be transported to the city's Los Rios district, where other stately old houses were located. Yet to Erin the house had been home for almost all her life. The thought of driving by and seeing it somewhere else was wrenching. It might possibly be turned into one of those quaint bed-and-breakfasts or a collectable shop with tourists traipsing through the rooms. She groaned inwardly.

Erin thought about the dismal prospects while she made coffee in the sunny kitchen. Her father hurried in and slammed the screen door back against the wall, his boots leaving a fine dusting of dirt on the worn linoleum.

"I found it," he shouted.

Erin turned around. "What?"

"That old lease you wanted to see." He looked proud of himself as he extended his big hand. "Open it and let's take a gander."

Taking the faded manila envelope, Erin's heart skipped a beat. She hurriedly scanned the document's dull print, then let out a whoop and grabbed her father around the neck. He gave her a bear hug, then set her down, his feet planted far apart, a grin on his leathery face. "It's good, then?"

Erin squeezed the document close to her chest. "It's like Mrs. Fielding always said. This property is to be used for farming and related purposes only."

He smacked his forehead with the heel of his hand. "Can we hold 'em to it?"

"We'll certainly try. Coffee's ready. Pour yourself a cup. I've got to run along now and see Archer. Oh, he's going to just *love* this."

"Whoo-ee!"

Jordan happened to look out the office window in time to see Erin Fury march up the steps, her back ramrod straight.

Here comes the kickboxer, he groaned, wondering what drove this strong young woman. Not waiting for her frontal assault this time, he prepared himself— jacket buttoned, tie straightened, and chin up.

His secretary announced in a frazzled tone, "It's that Fury woman again. She insists on talking to you, Mr. Archer. I don't know what to do with her."

"Show Ms. Fury in, Mrs. Courtney."

She muttered about people who didn't make appointments and left.

Moments later, Erin advanced toward his desk, boots thumping on the tiled floor, her inner inferno seeming to be less pronounced this time. He couldn't help noticing her shapely jeans-clad legs. Her small nose had a slight upward tilt, her eyes more green than hazel. Smooth creamy textured skin covered her graceful cheekbones. A man could feel energized just being in the same room with a woman like her—if it weren't for that temper.

"Good morning," he said. "Won't you sit down, Ms. Fury?"

By the mercurial look on her face, this wasn't going to be a golden moment. He decided to take a more casual approach this time and slipped his hands in his pockets, waiting.

A small muscle twitched beguilingly at the corner of her mouth. "Thanks, no, Mr. Archer. I'll state my piece and be out of here. I brought over a copy of our original lease. Please read it carefully." She handed it over. "It will explain everything."

He took it from her, barely touching her fingers. Electricity zipped between them. He bent to read it. "This lease is no longer valid. Mrs. Fielding's son, who inherited the land, sold the property, not her. That, in essence, cancels the previous owner's mandate, unless stipulated in writing by the son. It wasn't."

Erin shifted her position, shoulders squared like a lady Marine. "You can think again. This college's actions are indefensible. And in the words of T. S. Elliot, there are no permanent defeats because there are no permanent victories." She stuck her chin out, letting him know she wasn't some illiterate bumpkin. "However, we intend to win this one, Mr. Archer."

Touché! "Perhaps I can help you find another place," he offered, racking his brain for an alternative. "I have a realtor friend who . . ."

"No half-gnawed bones, please," she broke in. "We don't want your help, thank you. You've *helped* us quite enough, already."

He laughed uneasily. "Aren't you being a trifle childish? This is a business transaction, pure and simple."

Erin's face turned crimson. "You just don't get it, do you?" she sneered.

"I wish I could help," he said. "However . . ."

She held up a hand. "You have no idea what our operation is all about. Why don't you come over and take a good look before you wipe us off the planet."

He was about to reply when she whipped around and thundered out.

So much for peaceful negotiations, he thought ruefully, and sat down. Her quick-witted repartee hinted at a high intelligence. For some reason he was attracted to her from the first moment they met, even if he couldn't understand why. The document lay on the desktop. Why not humor Erin Fury and let the board see the old lease, he figured.

Jordan didn't know what made him go over to the ranch several days later. The last thing he wanted was to get involved with someone as testy as Erin Fury. Maybe he was some sort of a masochist? But she had extended an invitation of sorts, hadn't she?

He opened the car door, scattering chickens, and slid out, glancing around the place. It looked clean but the buildings were old and weathered. A large, laid-back dog hardly lifted his head before settling back down beside the barn. Across the barnyard, Erin helped a young girl with a long ponytail to dismount. The child wore a helmet and braces on her legs. When Erin turned to Jordan, her look read anything but cordial.

He admired the way she wore those western clothes in her own singular way. Something caused him to want to figure her out. Sauntering over, he made an excuse that sounded flimsier than a worn-out four-cylinder engine.

"I thought I'd just have a look around," he said lamely, "as you suggested."

"I see. Well, this is our place. Have a good look. By all means take your time."

She didn't smile but turned her attention back to the child, making sure the girl's feet were firmly on the ground. Then Erin helped a boy mount. Jordan stood back and watched her guide the pony around the arena with a lead rope. The boy held on to the reins with some expertise.

Apparently Erin relished working with these children. She was all smiles and encouragement. For some reason Jordan had wanted to learn if there might be a softness and vulnerability buried somewhere in her fiery makeup. It was crazy, and he knew it, but now that he'd seen her on her own turf, he felt guilty about not renewing their lease.

Erin released the rope, letting the boy take full control. He looked happy.

"Okay, Josh, you're on your own. Remember what we practiced."

Seeing the handicapped child so self-assured moved some emotion deep inside Jordan. It felt special to see the boy in the saddle mastering the art of riding as he had done once himself. In the beginning, Jordan had hardly been aware of the ranch, let alone what the Furys worked to accomplish.

He caught up to her. "I'm impressed by what you've got going here."

"This is an important operation," she replied in a cool, reserved tone, not taking her eyes off the boy. "When these children ride, they strengthen muscles not commonly used. We have all sorts of things going on, like a youth equestrian team that meets here on Sundays. The kids learn to groom horses as well as ride. They have a good time under close supervision— just hanging out."

He could see she was swept up by her work, captivated by the children and their progress. "Sounds like a good program," he said.

She gave him a faint smile. "Some of the children take to the saddle before they can read and write. They lose themselves in these activities."

"They're gutsy kids," he said. "You've probably been riding since you could sit up straight."

"Just about."

Jordan stood there in the dirt like some silly adolescent, wondering what else he should say. Erin bewildered him, causing him to want to know a lot more about her. He was sure she had no idea how she affected him. Just being around her made him feel amped up.

The boy put the horse through its paces, then rode back to Erin, a glow on his bright face.

"You're a pretty good rider," Jordan told him, and patted the horse's long neck.

The boy thanked him.

Erin glanced up at her young student. "You did just fine, Josh."

Jordan liked the sincerity of Erin's smile. The boy obviously took to her praise and direction.

"Mr. Archer, meet Josh Whitefeather, my best rider."

The boy said hi, an inquiring, if not too friendly look in his dark eyes.

"Glad to meet you," Jordan said.

Josh's eyes narrowed suspiciously. "You're that college president who wants to make the Furys move away."

Erin coughed. "Go ahead and ride Ol' Paint over to

the stables now, Josh. I'll be right behind you. Then you can help Stu rake hay."

Josh nodded. Jordan followed along. So the kid had rebuffed him. Funny how a child could make you feel like a heel.

When Josh passed by a tree, he leaned over and reached out to snatch a brown leaf that swirled on the breeze. Darn if the kid wasn't sure of himself in the saddle. Erin had taught him well. Jordan smiled.

Erin tethered the horse to a hitching post, then helped Josh down. With an unsteady gait, the boy wandered into the shadows of the stables. Erin pulled her gaze from him and turned to Jordan.

"Nice kid," he said.

"Josh is a trooper, all right. He has muscular dystrophy." Her eyes rounded. "What can I do for you?"

He looked at her, trying not to show his pleasure in finally being alone with her. What was this power she had over him? The attraction didn't make a lot of sense. They had only met less than two weeks before and she clearly hated his guts. Could any two people be more opposite—her the earth mother, him the driving force behind the college's expansion?

"I can see you're tremendous with kids," he said, not replying to the question.

"I try to be. Youngsters like Josh deserve the best. What they learn here will have a lasting effect on the kind of adults they'll become."

"I have no doubt."

"We need to give them reasons to feel good about themselves, just as your college does."

He got the message, and she was dead right, but he

only nodded. He could feel her pain, even if he was unable to do anything about it.

A middle-aged man wearing a straw cowboy hat huffed up to them, unsmiling. Silver-speckled sideburns framed his sun-lined face. Erin introduced Mike Fury, her father, to Jordan.

Fury's face flushed and his handshake faltered. "You the guy that wants to kick us off our land?"

"Actually, I did suggest it to the board. Wish I could say otherwise."

He caught the sudden disquiet on Erin's face. Did she think her father might pull back his fist and ram it into Jordan's nose? But the man kept a guarded countenance.

"I thought as much. Well, you might as well know it now, mister, you've got a fight on your hands." Fury turned away, giving him the cold shoulder, his eyes flint hard.

"Well," Erin said, coughing lightly, "I'll show you around, if you want. Although I don't know why, since you've already sent us those glad tidings. All this will be gone soon. Tell me, what's this spot we're standing on going to be, an ugly high-rise or a concrete parking lot?"

He didn't have an answer. Erin's russet-colored hair sparkled with red highlights in the sun. Not one stroke of makeup tinted her oval face. With her high color, she didn't need it. She had perfect skin and natural brows, with no artsy pencil arches. He asked himself why he noticed every little thing about her. This visit was supposed to be for business purposes.

"Did you show our lease to the board?" she asked in a forthright manner.

"I faxed a copy to Mr. Herrington, the chairman— yes."

"Well, we're making progress then." She hesitated a moment in an apparent attempt to keep down her irritation. "Oh, come on," she said. "I'll give you the grand tour as long as you're here."

He grinned. Inside the shaded interior of the stables, the smell of fresh hay and the pungent scent of horsehair favorably assailed his nostrils, reminding him of his youth. A brawny man, pushing thirty, dressed in torn jeans and a sweatshirt, stepped out of a stall and latched it behind him. He held something in his hand.

"Hi, Erin. I took care of Jupiter's welts. He ought to heal quick enough."

"Thanks, Stu." She introduced them. The man ignored Jordan's outstretched hand. "Don't forget about Aglow before you leave," she added.

"I'll be particularly patient. She's still frightened of us," he said.

"It takes time," Erin replied with compassion.

Stuart Wilson's mouth turned up in a crooked smile and he went about his business with only a slight nod to Jordan. However, Jordan caught the over-the-shoulder look of devotion he gave Erin once they started to walked on.

"Stu's a gem," Erin said, her voice low. "One of our remarkable volunteers. His family has a few acres down the road. Reminds me of my dad when he was younger. Stu seems to know intuitively how to gentle a horse."

Jordan felt a stab of jealousy. He peered over a gate

at a bay gelding. The stall had fresh hay spread around. The water trough was clear as glass.

"This horse came to us from a racetrack," Erin said. "They called him a hay-burner, since he hadn't won a race in six starts. The owner was ready to ship him off to a glue factory. Fortunately, California passed a law forbidding that sort of thing. We rescued him last week. He'd probably be run to death at some mediocre track if we didn't take him in. But he's beauty, isn't he?"

"Yes," he replied. The light sprinkling of freckles across the bridge of her nose intrigued Jordan. "Do you get many?"

"Not usually thoroughbreds—just saddle horses. People with one acre of land suddenly want to play cowboy. At first they like to see the horse standing right outside their sliding-glass door. Real picturesque. Then the manure draws flies and the rest is history. Horses are a lot of work. People don't realize just how much."

"What's this fellow's name?"

"Indian Man."

He heard the smile in her voice.

"What do you do with them after they're rescued? I've heard racehorses don't make good saddle horses." He liked the way her eyes lightened when he talked about the horse. She had a big heart.

"My father works with them. Most of our newcomers are terrified because they've been mistreated or neglected. Dad can gentle just about any horse. Never loses his temper, you see. And he rewards them with kindness like any good trainer worth his salt."

Jordan pointed to the horse in the next stall who

had hesitantly reached his elegant neck over the gate, extending his upper lip. "This one looks healthy."

"Like Indian Man, he's one of the luckier ones. We should find a good home for him soon enough. When they come to us they're frequently underfed and sick. It's pretty awful."

Jordan caught the little tremor in her voice. He stuffed his hands in his pockets. Why was he trying to close down this place? God, he'd put himself in an untenable position he wasn't quite sure he still believed in. Yet his loyalty was to the college. After all, they hired him.

Erin shot him a sidelong glance, then went on with a litany of just how they cared for horses. "We give them nourishing food, take care of injuries, and work to overcome their traumas."

"A big undertaking," he said earnestly. "I admire your operation here."

"Thanks."

He wanted to tell her about his youth living on a farm, but Mike Fury wandered up to them, grim-faced. He took something orange out of his pocket and handed it to Indian Man. Jordan watched the thoroughbred much on a carrot, its big teeth working methodically.

"That-a-guy," Fury said, stroking the horse's long, aquiline nose. His mouth quirked at Jordan. "Ever ride a horse?"

"Some."

Erin's father seemed like a sentimental man underneath his resentment for Jordan. In different circumstances, maybe they would have been friends. Jordan looked at the animal and smiled. He had a love for horses, himself, growing up with them on a vineyard in Sonoma County. But he thought the Furys wouldn't be interested.

"Fine thoroughbred," he said.

"Yeah, he's all right," Fury answered in a monotone.

Jordan shrugged. Like most men, he had his hopes and dreams, strengths and weakness. He'd always thought empathy was one of his strong suits, but in the last few years things had changed. He would catch himself setting some of his values aside in favor of goals. Or at least he always believed he was one of the good guys. He also thought himself sharp, too, but now he wasn't so sure. How could he undo the hasty decision he'd made about this ranch? The trustees would label him wishy-washy.

Jordan turned in time to catch the edge of Fury's scowl. It rankled, and he felt another twinge of guilt. He couldn't blame the man for his anger. Jordan would undoubtedly feel the same way, given a similar situation.

When they left the stables together, the Furys were courteous but not friendly. What had Jordan expected? Still, he was profoundly moved by all that he'd seen. And, down deep, he knew he'd have to fight his attraction to Erin Fury if he were to keep his focus and objectivity.

"Thanks for the tour. Appreciate it," he said.

Fury touched a finger to his broad brimmed hat, the veins standing out in his neck. "Anytime." He walked away with a trenchant stride.

Jordan had the distinct impression the man didn't like having him poke his nose around the ranch.

Erin crossed her arms over her chest, her eyes somber. "You can see we do important work here."

Jordan smiled. Not receiving one back, he lifted his shoulders. "You've convinced me."

A large tomcat appeared and wrapped its body around her ankle, then swiveled its head to stare at Jordan with distrustful jade eyes. Erin reached down and picked the cat up in her arms.

Jordan thanked her and hopped in his car, his mind in a quandary. He wanted to say he'd put in a good word for them, but how could he do that? Here he was, on the verge of bulldozing this land and turning it into more urban sprawl, but his heart was no longer in it.

Erin returned to Archer's office two days later. When she learned from the secretary that he wasn't in, she chastised herself for not calling first.

"You might make an appointment next time," the woman said curtly.

"I'll call for sure. But this is very important. When will he be back?"

"I can't say for sure."

Disappointed, Erin was about to turn away when a student-helper with tinted glasses and hair down to her waist, looked up from a file. "I saw Dr. Archer playing tennis a little while ago." She told Erin where to find the courts before the secretary swooped down on her to put the cabosh on giving out information.

Erin thanked the student, then hurried across the campus on foot. So Jordan Archer played tennis—and in the middle of the day. Smirking, she couldn't believe the man could pour water out of a boot without instructions pasted on the sole, let alone play tennis.

Turning the corner of a building, she spotted Jordan through a high chain-link fence. He wore white shorts and a matching polo shirt.

Pretty sporty, she thought with scorn. *Probably has dimples on his knees.*

He stood, knees bent, about to receive a cross-court serve. Bam! A perfectly executed return. She wished he'd missed the darned thing.

Erin slid open the gate to the enclosed court and stepped inside. Jordan reached up for the ball he'd just tossed for a serve and came down hard with his racket. The ball acquired a cannonball-splitting twist. His opponent, an attractive black-haired woman dressed in one of those little white skirts that shows off the legs to best advantage, smashed the return with equal power. What a forehand!

Erin leaned back against the fence, reticent now about interrupting the game.

Another serve. The woman made a deadly drop shot. Laughing, Jordan cried out in mock outrage when he couldn't reach it in time. Erin kept watching, spellbound, conscious of the way his well-muscled body moved with agile skill. Somehow, she'd wanted to think of him as puny under those expensive business suits.

On his next serve, the woman discharged a murderous return down the line in her favor. This time he didn't laugh. Regrouping, he glanced over at Erin in surprise. Then he swung. The ball soared high over the net and landed outside the back court. The second serve also landed out of bounds.

"Looking for me?" he said to Erin, his eyes flickering.

She gave him a slanted smile. "Yeah."

"Give me a couple of minutes to sew this up."

She glanced at her wristwatch, giving him a dismissive look. "Sure."

Archer lost the match. The woman threw up her hands in victory.

"I never thought I'd beat you in three sets," she said.

Erin hoped she hadn't distracted Archer, then asked herself why she should care. This was only a game. She had an important matter to discuss with him.

Archer jumped the net and shook the woman's hand in a congratulatory tradition. They sauntered off the court, smiling and making small talk. His walk had a cocky, self-satisfied clip to it.

Then, opening the gate for the woman, he said, "So long, Janis. Next week?"

"Same time." The woman beamed warmly, then walked on, her racket over a shoulder, a smile of satisfaction on her lips. She had hardly taken notice of Erin.

Archer strode up, toweling his neck and face.

"Your girlfriend?" Erin asked.

"Was once."

"Did she break up with you or did you get bored first?"

"Let's say it was mutual."

She could tell he didn't want to talk about it by the way he leaned down to re-tie his tennis shoe when it didn't need tying. But she prodded shamelessly anyway. "Did you get interested in someone else and she found out?"

"It's not a perfect world. Let's drop it, okay? You can play Dear Abby another time."

"How come you still play tennis with her? Let bygones be bygones?"

"Janis is a really good player. She's the women's tennis coach here. We were adult about the breakup."

"Your backhand needs work. It's all in the wrist action, you know."

Amusement etched the corner of his eyes. "It sucks, huh?"

"I've seen better."

"You play, then?"

"Used to. No time now."

He gave her a long, thoughtful look, making her feel off balance.

"I like to get out and unwind," he said.

"So you do your unwinding on the tennis court."

"At least once a week. Preferably two."

"Uh-huh."

He gave her a quick, bright smile. "I'll challenge you to a game sometime."

She didn't reply.

"What did you want to see me about?"

This time she didn't hesitate. "I wondered if you'd heard from the board. You must realize we're all really anxious over at the ranch."

"No, nothing. However, there might be a reply by now. Let's go to my office." He looked around. "Did you walk over?"

"I'm parked in front of your office building."

"Then I'll give you a lift."

Reluctantly, she accepted, and climbed into his BMW. Naturally, she told herself, what else would he be driving but a yuppie car? The leather upholstery smelled new and there were all kinds of gadgets on the dashboard. You'd have to be a rocket scientist to figure them all out. Maybe the car drove itself, she thought with disdain.

When they walked past Mrs. Courtney, the secretary acknowledged him but acted as though she didn't see Erin. The student was gone.

Archer sat down at the desk and turned on the computer. "Take a seat," he said. "Let me check on something first. Only take a minute."

She slid into a chair. "Mr. Archer . . ."

He didn't glance her way. She got up and scanned the monitor over his shoulder as he turned on his E-mail, well aware she was being rude.

"If you don't mind," he said.

Although disinclined, Erin took a seat.

Finally, he cleared his throat, his eyes fastening on hers. "No reply yet. You deserve an honest answer, Erin. Quite frankly, I doubt they'll relent."

He had used her first name but Erin didn't react. "The lease?" she rushed on, not about to let his 'I doubt' routine discourage her.

He shook his head.

Impatience nearly choked her as she fought to get the words out. "You can't use the land for anything except farming. Mrs. Fielding spelled it out plain as day."

He shrugged his shoulders. "It doesn't apply now. That was before her son sold the property to us. We've already gone over this. Remember?"

She breathed rapid, shallow breaths. Mustering her

most indignant voice, Erin said, "Mr. Archer, you're dog-wrong about this."

"I doubt it."

Erin bristled. He was so sure of himself. "We'll just see about that."

Pond scum! she wanted to scream at him as she left his office.

Chapter Three

J ordan drove back to the ranch a few days later. He'd already developed an affectionate curiosity for the goings-on there. The place was a sanctuary. Their pastoral way of life appealed to him, even if he had turned his back on such a life long ago. Only the night before in a dream, Erin's pretty face, surrounded by flying horses, had floated before his eyes like a lovely mirage.

His feet crunched on dead leaves when he slid from behind the wheel. Erin was at work in the stables when he found her, filling mangers with fresh feed. She looked radiant, her movements graceful. He called her name. She looked up, and seeing him, her smile faded.

"Hi," she said, going on with her activities. "What brings you over here? I would think you'd be behind that polished desk of yours pushing around important papers with a gold pen."

He ignored the caustic remark. "I thought I'd come by and tell you the board is willing to hear what you have to say at an informal meeting. Next Tuesday afternoon okay?"

The corners of her mouth turned up and her eyes widened. "You're kidding?"

A bug zapper toasted a fly and a horse snorted before he could reply.

"I'm not much of a kidder when it comes to important things."

She tossed him a guarded smile. "Maybe they finally see what I've been trying to tell you all along."

He didn't tell her he had argued valiantly for this opportunity, incurring the wrath of the trustees in the process. And he knew it probably wouldn't be much more than a courtesy meeting. Still, it pleased her. Who knew what might happen? Erin could be persuasive.

"That old lease has teeth in it," she said, a little triumph in her voice.

A gray horse stuck his head over the stall gate, making a chewing motion. Shreds of alfalfa hung out of the corners of its mouth. The musk smells of horses and feed filled the air.

"I ought to caution you not to get your hopes up, though."

"But at least they're willing to let us have our say." She leaned the pitchfork against a post. "When did you say all this is going to take place?"

"On the first, at four in the afternoon. Administration Hall boardroom."

She gave a short laugh. "Dad and I wouldn't miss it. The room better be big. We'll probably have supporters in the audience if word gets out."

There she goes, throwing around demands. Didn't she know what an informal meeting was? He didn't know whether to be irritated or to admire her tenacity.

"I'm finished here," she said, wiping her hands on her slim thighs. "Come on, I'll follow you out."

Was she trying to get rid of him? Probably.

Outside, he rested his forearms on a fence rail and admired the horses in the pasture. One in particular was taller than the others. His mane flickered like wind-whipped silk when he shook his head. His fine coat shone in the sunlight with a copper hue.

"That sleek bay's Indian Man, the racehorse, right?" Jordan said. "Seems you showed him to me last time I was here."

"I'm surprised you recognize him. We're not sure what we'll do with the big fella'. Too high-strung for the kids."

"Hum." He rubbed the slight nub of whiskers on his jaw. "That right?"

The gelding sauntered up to them. Erin let the horse smell her while it nuzzled the crook of her elbow. Then she gave him a small carrot she'd taken from a pocket. The horse munched with all the pleasure of someone eating chocolate cake. Jordan reached out and patted the long, velvety neck. The gelding's veined ears flicked forward and he nickered softly. Jordan wished he had some treat for the horse.

"Usually Indian Man doesn't like strangers," she said, "but he seems to accept you. I'm the only one who's ridden him so far. Quite an experience. The horse mistook me for a jockey and thought he was at the starting gate." Her mind seemed to drift elsewhere for a moment, and she added, as though to herself, "There has to be a harmony between horse and rider or it won't work."

"I heard something about that," he said. "The Horse Whisperer theory."

She let her attention focus on him. "I'm hoping to get Indian Man more conditioned to people. With younger horses, we start bonding right away, but these rescued horses haven't usually had that advantage."

"I'd like to buy him," Jordan said flat out.

Erin's mouth flew open. "You're putting me on."

"Actually, I'm not."

"What do you know about horses?" She sounded skeptical.

"A little."

"Oh? Like what? Tell me, you put two bucks on a filly to win at the races once, right?" She chuckled. "Seriously, if you try to put your behind on Indian Man, he'll run off with you. Might stop when he gets to the Mexican border if he's winded enough."

Jordan smiled, refusing to take offense. "Think about it."

Amazed, Erin half expected him to retract the offer or at least try to justify it. A frog ribitted in a juniper bush and the horse shifted away. Her mare rolled over in the dirt, then rose to stand on all fours, shaking herself, dust spiraling.

The familiar scene caused Erin to feel emotional, a reminder of what they were about to lose to this man standing beside her. Why, she wouldn't sell this horse to him if her life depended on it. But then, the gelding's life just might depend on Jordan taking him if they couldn't find someone else soon.

"I'll think about your offer," she said grudgingly. "But if we have to move, just where do you intend to board him? On the tennis court?"

"I don't have to make that decision this minute, do I?"

She shrugged. "I guess not."

The dun mare ambled over and threw her head up. Nervous, she stamped her hoof in the loose dirt, snorted, then trotted around in a wide circle.

"That's my Angel Face. Look at those big, wistful, nut-brown eyes. She's practically begging me to take her for a good, long run," Erin said. She reached out and gently scratched the course hairs on the horse's lower lip.

"Maybe we could ride together sometime," he offered.

She was about to say, *not on you life*, but wavered. "Tell you what. If you're really interested in Indian Man, I'll need to see if he'll let you ride him."

Sure the horse wouldn't, some devilish quirk in her wanted the gelding to make a fool out of this cityslicker-type with his shiny shoes and clean fingernails.

"Tomorrow morning, then?" he asked

"Six sharp."

He hesitated, raised a thick eyebrow, and nodded. "I'll be here."

Jordan arrived at the stables, unshaven, his eyes barely open. He saw that the horses had already been saddled and tethered to a hitching post in front of the barn. Indian Man stood with a hind leg bent slightly, in a resting position. The horse swished his tail, dislodging a pesky horsefly. Angel Face leaned over and nibbled his withers as a dust devil whipped along the ground.

By the time Jordan popped the car door open, Erin had come out of the stables and was slipping something into a saddlebag. She gave him a half-hearted wave as he strolled toward her. She walked around the horses, checking tack. Her movements had a certain classic dignity, even in the faded blue jeans she wore so well. Although he didn't like her standoffish ways, he accepted them. What did she really know about him? Nothing, other than he was president of Regency College and had abruptly created a lot of mayhem in her life.

He held off telling her he was interested in animals and open spaces. Thinking of himself as a caring person, he didn't usually toss people off their land, either, contrary to what she thought. But it was out of his hands now, and he knew she wouldn't want to hear any excuses. She undoubtedly thought of him as a selfish, thoughtless, arrogant fool. Hadn't she made that perfectly clear?

He glanced around. Blackbirds silently observed them, perched on telephone wires like notes on a musical staff. Already the morning was dazzlingly superoxygenated. He took a deep breath, filling his lungs with clean, dewy air. This had to be the earliest he'd been up in years. It reminded him of why he didn't want to be a farmer like his father.

"Nice morning for a horseback ride, Erin."

"Yeah." Her reply lacked any sign of enthusiasm as she finished preparations.

A fat tabby jumped down from a fence post and meowed. Jordan had seen the cat lurking around before. Nearby, a red hen cackled when the cat got too close to her chicks and she ran him off, raising a commotion.

Dressed in new jeans and a gray college sweatshirt, Jordan mounted Indian Man with a host of misgivings. The horse pinned his ears back and sidestepped but didn't bolt. Jordan heaved a sigh of relief, hoping Erin didn't notice his slight agitation. Indian Man pranced in a wide circle, his head held high.

Erin placed her foot in the stirrup and swung into the saddle with a smoothly elegant ease. She kept a watchful eye on him. He came close to telling her he wasn't one of the kids.

Like two adversaries, they let the horses canter down the rutted road, the horses' hooves clattering and kicking up dust. So far so good, he thought. At least he was still in the saddle.

Soon, they skirted the colorful historic hamlet of San Juan Capistrano, with its famous mission and quaint shops, the doors not yet open for business. With Erin in the lead, they followed a plume of sunlight along the Ortega Highway until they passed housing developments with clipped hedges and emerald green lawns. The neighborhood shouted of two income families.

Jordan let his horse move up beside hers. They traveled along a maze of trails leading toward the scenic Cleveland National Forest. Crossing the edge of a ranch, Jordan saw a black bull in a pasture. It raised its powerful head and snorted, rattling the chain around a massive neck as it scuffed the ground. Jordan didn't make eye contact, having no desire to play matador. They rode on in silence.

Finally, Erin spoke. "I love the magic of spring, its renewal of life."

"Yeah," he replied lightly. "Makes me want to get out more often."

In a little while Erin and Jordan found themselves surrounded by fragrant purple sage. When they reached a rain-flushed creek filled with green reeds and partly submerged mossy stones, the horses stopped and lowered their heads to drink in gulps of cool water. A sycamore dipped down at the water's edge, its leaves dancing on the bubbling current.

"How did you get into working with horses and kids?" he asked offhandedly.

"My dad had a vision twenty years ago to breed horses, but interest in them was already waning here in the valley. The ranches were being sliced up even then and sold off to developers. One thing led to another, I guess. The ranch we lease was triple the size at that time. We raised strawberries, as well as the oranges. Mrs. Fielding's son talked his mother into selling off more than half of the acreage when her husband passed away. But she swore she'd never sell the remaining twenty acres," Erin said.

"Did your father ever try to buy the land?"

"Dad made offers early on. Mrs. Fielding refused, couldn't bear to part with it, she told him, even though she hadn't lived on the place for years."

"I see."

They rode on. Erin didn't say more.

"Indian Man's not bad to ride," Jordan said to change the subject. He cast an admiring eye over the gelding. "Just a trifle skittish."

Erin's mood lightened and she grinned. "Looks like you've developed something mystical between you."

With the next breath, she grasped the topic of conversation by the reins and ran it directly down the trail she wanted to go.

"Finding homes for horses isn't easy," she said. "There aren't that many ranches left. Nor places to board them, either. You'll really be doing our community a disservice if you move ahead with your preposterous plans to close us down."

"No doubt you believe unswervingly in what you do, Erin. That's commendable. But so do we."

She ignored his comment. "People haven't always been good to horses. Historically, when the poor animals can't work anymore, their owners cast them off like so much rubbish. We try hard to reverse that kind of abuse. As for the disabled children, riding teaches them respect, patience and discipline, and gives them a sense of self."

"You're one heck of a dedicated lady. I admire your unflagging belief in making changes in those kids' lives."

She looked at him, as though her thoughts were somewhere else. "Thanks. To me, there is no other way."

The more he learned about Erin Fury, the more he admired her. Being on the ranch was like being caught up in a time warp.

Yeah, she's mother earth, all right. This woman

eats, sleeps, and talks horses—either that or kids. She's a regular modern day Good Samaritan.

"What do your volunteers do, exactly?" he asked, thinking of the guy she'd spoken to earlier. "Stuart, wasn't it?"

She tilted her chin and her eyes softened. "They're good-hearted people who come to the ranch and dive right in, mucking out stalls, grooming horses or pushing a broom. Some help with the kids, too. This is everyone's riding school—a community affair."

He listened patiently, understanding that she wanted him to know just what a dastardly deed he and the board members were about to do. Well, as it happened, he didn't need a lot of convincing anymore. Still, his hands were tied. The trustees had the final say in the matter.

They crossed into a small valley lined with vivid blue chia plants. A strong breeze blew the long, wild grass into a shag-like carpet. Although they weren't far from civilization, traveling through the canyons and meadows was like stepping into a gentler world, that is, until Jordan's horse began to fidget.

Erin stood up in the stirrups, her hand shielding her eyes, and scanned the hills around them. Jordan saw the mountain lion even before Erin discovered it and quietly pointed. The magnificent beige cat shimmered like a phantom in the glare of the morning sun. It quietly observed them from the advantage of a cave opening, its eyes wary.

"Let's move ahead," Erin whispered. "They don't usually pay any attention to people but why tempt fate."

Jordan glanced back over his shoulder. The mountain lion had disappeared. He breathed a little easier.

Further on, they switched to a different trail higher in the hills. Jordan asked casually, "What do you do for fun, Erin? What sort of things make you happy?"

He prided himself with his straightforwardness, his sense of order. Yet the jarring arguments of this woman so mesmerized him, he wasn't himself. Being with her was like taking Humanities 101.

She turned in the saddle and looked at him, very circumspect. "Haven't I been telling you?"

He cleared his throat. "Why, sure. Of course. It was an idiotic question."

"You still don't get it, do you? Our ranch must be saved because it is a rare, unspoiled spot amid creeping suburban sprawl. It was here before the college was built and it'll remain, just like it is today, in spite of your plans."

Not a diamond day, he thought, leaning back in the saddle and stretching his legs. Erin had a way of tweaking his nose. Every time he tried to get her to lighten up, she started in on her problems. She probably thought he was the Creature from the Black Lagoon. To her, the place was *Mayberry*. He half expected to be introduced to Andy Griffith and Opie.

However, she had let him ride Indian Man—a considerable concession. She looked at him and smiled. It made him feel good, even if it was a bit cool. The horses came to another brook and crossed over, whipping up silver crystal-clear water around their knees.

In truth, Jordan hadn't ridden in years. The immutable rhythm of the big horse's movements reminded him of his youth. Erin had said the gelding would run away, but the big guy was almost as relaxed as an old nag once they had gotten beyond the traffic. No creaking starting gates out here to rile him. Jordan stared thoughtfully ahead at the chaparral-covered hills.

This is about as good as it gets, he thought. *It couldn't be more beautiful.*

Turning to Erin, he said, "Two people can look at the exact same thing and see something wholly different, Erin. For instance, I see your land going for more student housing. No matter how you slice it, there are always two sides to an issue. And neither are totally bad."

Erin felt the storm clouds gather in her mind. Naturally, the man would think that way. What else? It was to his benefit. But she made herself calm down, knowing that it's a lot easier to react than it is to think something through. And that's exactly what she'd done in his office—overreacted. Yet she knew she couldn't trust this man, even if he seemed to be leaning slightly in their favor now. Hadn't he, in a matter of days, destroyed their peace of mind, threatening their way of life?

The sky blanched with summer-like heat and the breeze rattled leaves from the wild oak trees. She recalled her dream the night before when trees suddenly went from stately statues to green dragons spitting fire. Oh, she was experiencing some doosies lately.

Erin shifted in the saddle, the faint sliding sound of the fabric of her jeans murmuring off the leather. She glanced at Jordan. He sat well on his mount. His sculptured face and white teeth marked him a handsome man, and his powerful thighs in the Wranglers reminded her of a stallion. Forcing the intimate thoughts away, she shook her head with regret. The man was, after all, the enemy.

In spite of herself, Erin's thoughts continued to linger on him. She remembered how Jordan had absorbed the vindictive words she'd hurled at him in his office without telling her to get lost. That took stamina.

Years ago Erin's mother had advised her to modulate her tone of voice. "Don't create more rancor when you want to win an argument."

Why couldn't she do that? Erin was definitely too much like her father, she told herself. But the train wreck, by way of the letter, had already occurred. Did it really matter how she spoke her piece anymore?

She glanced at Jordan. How had she come to think of him as Jordan and not Archer? There was something impressive about him. Only days before he had been the stuffed-shirt in the suit and tie. Now he wore jeans and boots most attractively. And so far he managed the racehorse with relative ease. The man, however, was some sort of a chameleon and she confessed to not having a handle on him yet.

They crested a steep hill and looked down at a flower-strewn meadow.

"Let's rest the horses," she said. "I brought along lemonade. You must be thirsty. I am."

"You're right about that. My throat feels like a dust bowl."

Jordan could feel his shoulder joints stiffen and get sore from hunching over the saddle, not to mention his backside, when he climbed off the horse. They'd been traveling for going on two hours. He glanced at Erin as she dismounted. A warm pang circuited through him. Then Indian Man raised his head, quirked his ears forward, and sniffed the air, distracting Jordan. Could the mountain lion be tracking them? Not seeing any sign of the big cat, he said nothing.

They tethered the horses to a low oak branch. Erin gazed with satisfaction at the thick, course grass and multicolored flowers. "This place is so gorgeous at this time of year. It's my favorite spot in all the world."

"I can understand why. Do you ride out here often?"

"Not nearly as often as I'd like. Things get pretty hectic on the ranch."

She took a thermos and two plastic mugs out of the saddlebag and found a place for them near a big log lying on the grass. But neither of them sat down. A butterfly flew around her head, then skittered off. Erin poured the pale yellow liquid into mugs and handed one to him.

"Thanks."

"Let's sit down," she said.

"Funny, I didn't realize we were standing."

Erin grinned. His penetrating eyes were on her as he seated himself and leaned his back comfortably against the log. Erin perched beside him on top of it and bent to pick a brilliant, cerise wildflower. She examined the finely formed bud. The infinite blue sky warmed her spirits and she put aside her cares and worries and let herself enjoy the calm, tranquil meadow.

All at once a hawk made an enormous swing skyward, cawing noisily. Erin looked up in time to see a squirrel dart across a limb, moving higher.

Then she heard the bloodcurdling clamor of the mountain lion. "It's close," she murmured. "Too darn close."

Terrified, Indian Man jerked back on the reins, his eyes ablaze with fear, and easily broke away in his agitation. Erin tried to catch the reins but they slipped from her hands like wet noodles. She raced to retrieve her .22 from its saddle sheath.

Jordan lunged for the thoroughbred's reins, grabbed them and held on for dear life. The horse dragged him roughly sideways, then spun around. He managed to get on his feet and dig in the heels of his boots, shouting, "Whoa!"

Everything happened in a split second. Erin fired the rifle into the sky to frighten away the mountain lion. The sound echoed off the chambered walls of the canyon like canyon fire. Jordan held on to the powerful horse, making a valiant effort to keep him from dashing away. The gunfire only made matters worse. Erin ran up and grasped the horse's halter to help subdue him. Still quivering, the gelding slowly calmed down. She spoke reassuring words. Angel Face appeared only mildly troubled by the whole incident.

"Whew! That was close," Jordan said. "I could see the color of its eyes."

Erin looked at Jordan with admiration. "We almost lost a horse. And for a minute I thought I might lose you, too. Are you okay?"

He dusted himself off. "I'll be fine as long as that mountain lion doesn't make a return call. Hey, you're quite an Annie Get Your Gun."

"I don't think I'd ever have the heart to shoot anything, but it scares critters away. That cat is probably miles from here by now. And I'm quite sure he'll be looking for something more exciting to do than to track us."

"Did you know the cat was following?"

"I had a pretty good hunch."

"Why didn't you mention it?"

"Why borrow trouble?"

Jordan patted Indian Man's flanks, then led him around in a circle to get the danger off the horse's mind and let his adrenaline settle.

When things got back to normal, Erin glanced in the distance at the highest peak she could see in the Cleveland National Forest, thinking about Jordan. This man certainly astonished her with his quick actions. He wasn't any tenderfoot.

Erin stroked Angel Face's long nose, then set about loosening her girth. Jordan did the same, making sure both horses were secured to a stronger tree branch this time. She came back and sat down on the grass next to him. He plucked a blade of grass and stuck it between his teeth, grinning.

"I know you like to talk about the animals and the children who come to the ranch, but what about you?"

"Me? What do you mean?"

"Like what do you do during your private time—your days off?"

She couldn't help but be amused. Hers was not an eight to five job. "I don't take any days off. We're too busy."

"C'mon. What do you like to do? See a movie now and again—go dancing?"

She leaned back. They were nearly shoulder to shoulder. "Maybe take a leisurely bubblebath or read a good book when I have some free time—which isn't often. Most of all, I like to come out here where it's

quiet and peaceful. I can shed my worries, set aside
my sense of self—just be one with nature."

"So you brought me to your favorite location. I'm
honored."

It was true. But why had she? Out of his office, he
seemed personable and buoyant, like a different man.
Maybe that was the reason.

"How about you?" she asked. "Ever want a different
career?"

He shrugged indifferently. "Tell me, Erin, did you
never want anything else for yourself?"

She shook her head. "Nope."

He puckered his lips and threw away the blade of
grass. "It must be great to know what it is you want."

"And you don't? You're pretty young to be a college president."

"It's a small college."

"You haven't told me how you got your position."

"I attended Stanford—on a scholarship—then finished up my Ph.D."

"And?"

"I did my post-doctoral in business administration.
One thing led to another, I guess."

"You must have more degrees than a thermometer,
judging from the one's I saw on your office wall."

He gave a belly laugh. "Hardly."

"I dropped out of college in my junior year. Dad
needed me. I've never regretted it, though," she said
a bit too defensively. "If you weren't doing your president thing, what then?"

He held off divulging his private thoughts and made
a joke of it. "A rodeo rider."

She laughed. "You mean ride broncos or one of those mean, ornery bulls?"

He noticed one of her teeth appeared to have been chipped at some time. From falling off a horse, maybe? "Goats," he replied.

She gave him a wide grin. That seemed to go down well, he thought.

A blue jay called and was answered by another bird.

Erin said, "We ought to be going."

"Already?"

Erin scrambled to her feet and reached tapered fingers through her hair, pushing it back from her face. He joined her, thinking he'd like to remain longer in the meadow, get her to talk a little more about herself.

She returned the thermos and mugs to the saddlebags. Miss efficient.

He wondered what she thought of him—really thought of him—not counting the ranch/dorm issue. Did she mention his name in a condescending tone to friends, sneer when she discussed him? He couldn't blame her if she did.

Erin turned in time to catch him off-guard. "Well, how do you like the horse?"

"Fine. He's confident and has an easy gait. A trifle high-strung, though. But you did warn me. However, I feel comfortable with him."

"You've never . . . uh . . . mistreated an animal, have you?" she asked straight out.

The set of her mouth made him think anyone who had was two degrees below a cockroach.

"God, no!" he blurted.

She went on scrutinizing him in a none too subtle

way. "Maybe you don't want him, after all. He can be a problem."

"I want him, all right. He and I are already buddies."

"You haven't said where you plan to keep him."

He grinned. "How about if I just board him at your stables?"

She scoffed. "Very funny. Have you forgotten you're evicting us?"

"I've been meaning to tell you something all morning, Erin. I sent your lease to the board, as I said I would, and I'm trying to get them to overturn their decision." He felt pleased with himself.

She stared at him, suspicion written all over her pretty face, and her mouth gave a nervous twitch. "On the level?"

"On the level, Erin."

She cleared her throat and looked away for a moment, then gazed back at him. "I don't know. We need to be confident our horses will go to good homes."

The jump shift in subject threw him. Was she dismissing all his efforts?

"Maybe I'm wrong about you," she said, her voice slow and thoughtful. "Maybe you're for real and want to undo this mess. However, I'm not ready to trust you yet, Jordan Archer."

She tapped her fingers on the saddle horn. He felt bad, hearing the unexpected tremor of sadness in her tone, and her vulnerability touched him. She wasn't half the firebrand she portrayed herself to be.

"Give me a little time to work this all out," he said.

"Time isn't something we've got a lot of," she replied.

He wanted to reach out and pat her hand to reassure

her. Strange, this attraction. Instead, he gave her a stalwart smile. She was the kind of woman who made the prospects of getting lost out here highly desirable.

"We better go," she said.

He glanced at his watch. "Yeah." Thinking they'd only be gone for an hour or so, he'd already missed a meeting, but he wasn't going to bring it up.

Erin leaned down to check Angel Face's right hoof, revealing several inches of creamy backside between her shirt and jeans. He itched to touch her skin, embrace her. Then she straightened. Slightly delirious, he took in a sharp breath. Catching him looking at her, her eyes rounded, and he found himself squinting up at a passing cloud.

She prepared to mount, and he hurried to her side.

"Let me give you a leg up," he offered.

She turned to him, her lips as soft as velvet petals. A rocket exploded in his brain. In an instant, Jordan's mouth covered hers, confidently persuasive, searing.

Erin's mind reeled. Unable to move, she stared into those slate-gray eyes, her wall of restraint shifting unsteadily. When he let her go, a surge of emotion undulated over her, leaving her emotions fragile. The corners of his eyes creased and he inhaled with a jagged breath. She stepped back against the horse's side before she succumbed to the adoring look on his face once more.

"Maybe we could meet somewhere later," he said, his voice husky, as their lips parted. "We could have a bite to eat—discuss..uh . . . Indian Man."

A buzz saw went off in her head and she gazed at him with complete resistance, shaking her head. She had actually been thinking how nice it would be. A real date. And his kisses had flattered her. "I don't think that's a good idea," she replied.

His eyes flickered. "Don't give up on me yet, Erin. You may find I'm not such a bad guy."

When he grasped her waist and helped her mount, she experienced a jittery flutter, like being in a plane taking off too fast. She had to admit to a physical attraction to this man. But anything else was absurd, wasn't it?

They rode back along fire roads and coyote paths, taking a different route, with no sign of the mountain lion anywhere near.

When they arrived back at the ranch, her father was leaning against the barn doorframe, arms over his massive chest. He cut his gaze toward Jordan, the wrinkles on his brow deepening. "I see you made it back in one piece," he trumpeted. "Been gone long enough. Thought about sending out a posse."

Erin knew that angry gaze. It said, *What the Sam Hill are you doing riding off with Jordan Archer?*

She should have told him about going riding with Archer, rather than just leaving a note on the table.

"Morning, Mr. Fury," Jordan said. "Great day for a ride."

Her father mumbled, a cantankerous expression mapping his face.

Erin flashed her father a quick smile. "Hi, Dad. Jordan's interested in buying Indian Man. Can we discuss it later?"

His eyes snapped, but he gave in. "Yeah, later."

Her father took out a cigarette, lit it and inhaled deeply. Erin felt sick inside. Supposedly, he'd given up the dead weed habit over a month ago. She worried about his health.

He turned his back and strode into the barn without looking at either of them, smoke trailing.

Jordan dismounted. "Hey, I barbecue a faultless steak. How about letting me prove it to you, Erin?"

"I don't think so," she said, her voice an octave too high. Coming back to the ranch was like a reality check. She wouldn't put her faith in someone like Jordan Archer, even if she couldn't deny he appealed to her on a certain level.

He shrugged a shoulder and his mouth turned down. "Thanks for the ride. And about the horse . . . he will do just fine. I'll be getting back to you soon."

He tied the horse's reins to a hitching post, unfastened the saddle and slipped it off, depositing it on a bench. Then he sauntered to his sporty BMW without so much as a glance back and drove away.

Both men had turned their backs on her, and Erin didn't like it very much. Maybe she should take Jordan up on his offer, work a little harder to persuade him to change his mind. Wasn't she being shortsighted?

Chapter Four

Spending the previous day with Jordan left a favorable impression of Erin, although she tried to put it out of her mind. Weren't they at opposite ends of the galaxy—water and oil, yin and yang? Still, their hours together had given her the warm fuzzies. She never dreamed she'd spend more than five minutes with the man without wanting to tear his head off.

Seated behind the desk in her rustic office chair, Erin hoped no one would walk in until she had a better grasp of what it all meant. Okay, Jordan was good-looking, interesting, sharp, and he seemed to be interested in everything she had to say. Those were certainly pluses, since most of the men she'd gone out with wanted to do all the talking. Yet where could it lead? Absolutely nowhere. She couldn't believe she was having these thoughts about him in the first place. What was wrong with her? Could she be making him into a nice guy because of some inner need? God forbid.

C'mon, Erin, get a grip.

No, she would simply go on with her life, minus the man. However, that might not be so easy. Jordan didn't appear to be the kind who took no for an answer. It was the first time she'd met someone she cared about in a long time. And he apparently wanted to buy the thoroughbred. Perhaps that was his real motive in coming around, and not some interest in her. A plain saddle horse wouldn't do for a man like Jordan Archer. Could she let him have Indian Man, knowing he and his associates were forcing them off the land?

Folly. Pure folly.

Erin made up her mind to forget the whole thing and get busy with the depressing task of making phone calls. Placing her finger on the Rolodex, she thought of all the people she'd need to notify. Beginning with the 'A's,' she thumbed through the cards on the desk with a heavy heart.

Erin punched in the first set of numbers and waited until a familiar voice came on the line. "Adele? This is Erin Fury. Yes, I'm fine. But I have bad news, I'm afraid. No, Dad's also fine. It's our lease, you see. The new property owners won't renew it." She listened glumly for the shocked reply. "We're devastated, too. It could mean we might have to shut down our operations. You'll be getting a newsletter from us. Right— just terrible. We'll do everything we can to fight their decision, but I have to be honest, it doesn't look good."

By the time Erin worked through the first half of the list, it was noon. Food was the furthest thing from her mind. Her throat felt as dry as the Mojave desert. She took a bottle of spring water out of the small refrigerator, twisted off the cap, and swallowed a long, cool drink.

Sarah Whitefeather knocked lightly and opened the office door. Erin hadn't heard her drive in. Sarah flicked her dark hair back and smiled, her round, friendly face curious. "Hi," she said. "You look like your jaw's about to drop in your lap. Bad time, huh?"

"Mmm. You could say that. Let's go up to the house. I've got to get out of these four walls."

They strolled outside. The sun ducked behind a billowing cloud, shadowing the surroundings. Erin told her friend about the sad calls she had just finished making. "Some of them weren't home and I just couldn't leave a message like that on their answering machines."

Sarah nodded in sympathy. "It's a darn shame."

In the kitchen, Erin put on a pot of coffee. "I don't know what to make of Jordan Archer. In truth, he's hard to dislike. I let him ride Indian Man yesterday. Being with him out there in the back country gave me a different slant on him. He's not so bad away from that campus. And he said he's trying to get the trustees to reconsider, although I'm not sure I believe him." She omitted the part about the kisses.

"Then he can't be too bad."

"I get a sense that he regrets what he did."

"I met Jordan once at one of the mission doings," Sarah said with a sly smile, "a Native American powwow. How unfair for men to have such long eye-lashes."

Erin sat down at the table across from her friend. "What did you really think of him?"

Sarah tilted her head. "In so many words the man is suave, sophisticated, and terribly attractive. He has the chiseled good looks of a movie star."

"Oh, c'mon. He's not that handsome."

"Could be Mr. Right in disguise."

"Well, he's not my 'Mr. Right,' if that's what you're thinking. You know I never cared for those polished types," Erin said coolly.

Sarah shot her a mischievous gaze. "I never suggested he was. Personally, though, I think he's awesome."

Erin fidgeted with a broken fingernail. "I've got so much on my mind these days. I can't be thinking about me."

Sarah shrugged and let the comment slide. "What are you going to do? There's not much open space left around here to start up a new ranch."

"We're not caving in yet. Dad and I intend to launch a tough campaign to keep this place."

Sarah brightened. "What can I do? I love a good fight."

"If the trustees turn us down at the coming meeting, we'll try to get the community behind us."

"At least Jordan seems to be trying, Erin. I had the impression he leaned toward the naturalist viewpoint," Sarah said, "from the way he talked about protecting mountain lions in the hill country."

Erin chuckled. "He almost came face to face with one. The big cat tracked us through the canyons and sneaked in close enough to spook Indian Man. Jordan had to take a flying leap to grab the reins before the horse ran off. I have to admit he did a pretty good job of handling the high-strung racehorse."

"So he's not just a desk jockey."

"Apparently he has talents I was not aware of."

"A mystery man. Interesting. But don't let him try to schmooze you."

Erin laughed, cutting across her friend's next words. "Back to our current battle. We might even get the newspaper involved—you know, a human interest story."

"They'll love it. Why not hold a big rally? Invite everyone. Their college students, too. It'll make those trustees, including Archer, look bad. Serve him right."

"The more people we can get to turn out for it, the better."

"Make sure you have plenty of alternative plans," Sarah said. "I wouldn't trust them until you have a new lease on paper."

Erin nodded. She glanced out the window. Her father was removing wilted flowers from the vibrantly colorful garden. He stooped to inhale the fragrance of a red rose. Then he turned to prune the overgrown climber on the split-rail fence surrounding the garden. She hadn't seen him out there for quite some time.

"Dad used to take delight in his garden," she said wistfully. "Mom's death changed all that. I wonder if he'll ever be his old self again."

Sarah sympathized. "It's tough to see him so down-hearted."

Erin rose from the table and poured coffee into

brown mugs covered with tiny daisies. "It'll kill him if we have to move from this place."

The wall telephone rang. She hurried across the room and grabbed it. "Fury Ranch. Erin speaking."

She almost dropped the receiver. Jordan Archer smoothly identified himself and asked her to meet him for lunch the next day. Her hands felt sweaty, her throat tightened, and her head spun.

"I'm awfully busy," she said in a stuttery voice.

"We need to talk, you and I."

"About the horse—oh, yes. I think we can sell him to you but . . ."

"Let's say one o'clock Saturday. Dana Point Marina. Okay?"

"Well . . ."

"I'll meet you at the Beach House."

"Uh . . ."

"See you then." He hung up.

Erin glanced at Sarah, feeling like an idiot. "I didn't handle that very well, stammering that way, did I?"

Sarah chuckled. "You, the sure shooter? I wouldn't think so. That had to be Jordan, and he wants to take you somewhere, right? That's not so bad, Erin. What can it hurt? Maybe you'll get lucky and talk him into having the trustees scuttle that crazy idea. Don't be afraid to try all the angles, ol' girl."

"If you're hinting at what I think you're hinting, you can just forget it."

Sarah held up her palms, face out. "Who me? Never. Well, if you're not going to offer me a sandwich to go with the coffee, I'd best head back to work."

Erin jumped up. "I've got cheese. Will that be do?"

"Thanks. Sounds great. But no mayo, just mustard. I'm watching my weight."

On Saturday, a ton of traffic clogged the streets in San Juan Capistrano as Erin drove to the marina a few miles down the road. She entered the restaurant, already twenty minutes late, and glanced around. Jordan didn't see her at first. He stood by the reception desk in profile, a small, hard smile on his face.

When she called, "Jordan?" he turned, and the irritation quickly drained from him.

"There you are," he said.

"Sorry to be late. I got caught in traffic."

"No problem."

While they waited for the hostess to return, Erin looked around. A giant tank held exotic fish behind the reception desk. Pictures of fishermen and their catches hung on the walls.

A hostess, tall and willowy, seated them in captains chairs at a table beside the wide windows overlooking one of the channels. Waitresses passed by carrying plates of fresh, succulent-smelling seafood on platters. Erin noticed that nearly every table was occupied with patrons who looked relaxed and happy. Many of them were dressed in white slacks and shirts with anchors, gold ropes and stars or fish.

Moored boats bobbed in slips on the other side of the windows. People strolled on the sidewalk just below. A pelican swooped behind a boat tacking down the channel.

Erin opened a menu. "What do you recommend? It all looks good."

"Their Shrimp Louie."

"Mmm, sold. I'll try the shrimp, then."

He looked pleased and gave her a grin. "It better be outstanding today."

A waitress with short, straight hair pulled back in tiny barrettes across the front, came along and took their orders. When she left, Erin and Jordan sat quietly, trying not to stare at each other across the table. Erin wondered how to start the conversation, then asked herself why she had agreed to come.

"You look nice," he said. "Peach is your color."

Erin found herself blushing. "Thanks."

She'd carefully chosen white slacks, a peach-colored blouse and the turquoise jewelry Sarah and Josh had given her for Christmas.

Jordan's focus swung to the boat that was now maneuvering into a slip. The pelican had flown away. His slate-gray eyes flickered, seeming to acknowledge something she had no idea about. He wore chinos and a navy blue polo shirt open at the neck, revealing curly bronzed chest hair.

When he turned back, Erin asked, "I gather you still want Indian Man?"

"He's a terrific horse, and yes, I do want him."

"Shouldn't we be talking about a price then?"

"You name it. If it's a mill, forget it."

She chuckled. "Actually, I'll have to talk to Dad about it, but a million is a trifle high for a horse who's never won a race."

She still felt uncertain about parting with the racehorse. Due to the circumstances, Jordan was the last man she wanted to sell the gelding to.

"We'll sell him cheap," she conceded straight-away. "That's what we do. We're not out to make a pile of money—just place the horses with people who care." Then she looked at him closer. "We usually keep a check on them, though. You won't mind?"

"Not at all. I expect it." He cast admiring eyes over her.

"You know a lot about me, Jordan, but I know practically nothing about you. Were you raised around here?"

"No. I grew up on a vineyard in Sonoma County."

She listened, waiting for him to go on.

Hesitating, he began speaking in generalities. "It's good to see California wine is more popular than ever. Some time during the eighteen hundreds many of the French vineyards were wiped out—disease. They ordered cuttings from California. Interesting, wouldn't you say, since most of our grapes originally came from France."

Fascinated, her gaze dwelled on his while he told her of an incident when a fire nearly destroyed his family's ranch. "That was one horrible night. We were up for forty-eight hours straight. Neighboring farmers came to help. And there were fire engines everywhere. If I hadn't been so scared, those red engines would have mesmerized me, seeing as how I was only around twelve at the time."

She noticed how his eyes registered feelings she wouldn't have thought he possessed. For a little while he became lost in the flashbacks of his youth, and when he returned to the present, he seemed slightly embarrassed, ducking his head.

The waitress brought back a tray and they ate in near silence. Erin bit into a pink shrimp. It tasted delicious. "You were right," she said. "This is wonderful."

He smiled broadly.

When they finished, they lingered over coffee, in no hurry to leave.

Jordan looked thoughtful. "Memories of childhood sometimes have a mythical quality, I've heard people say. Maybe mine wasn't quite like I remember it."

"Mine was pretty normal, filled with horses and puppies and kittens all around. My mom was sweet and easy going. Dad was sterner, but only when he thought I might hurt myself," she said. "I guess you could say I was a tomboy."

"Actually, sometimes life was pretty chaotic in the Archer household. I have four sisters who wanted to mother me, and they seemed to always be in the bathroom doing things to their hair. My mother was sort of tense, with a heavy dose of superstition thrown in from her Basque ancestry."

"And your father?"

"A hard worker—sort of distant. Always busy out in the fields, preparing the soil, girdling grapevines, harvesting and trimming them back afterward. Mom's gone now."

"My mom, too. Sad."

"Yeah."

Jordan wondered why he was telling Erin all this, since it wasn't like him to reveal much of himself to people. When they first met he thought she was a fiery gal, but now he realized she had a protective shield. Underneath all that crust he found she could be vulnerable and sweet.

"Do you miss the smell of grapes at harvest time

and the wine-making?" she asked. "Did you stomp grapes in a big barrel and have parties when it was over?"

"Sure. All of the above. It meant home." He paused, overcome with nostalgia.

Erin continued to look at his face, waiting for him to continue, but he'd said plenty already. "Enough of me. I want to hear more about you."

Jordan reached out and took her hand, giving it a slight squeeze. The texture of her skin was soft and satiny. He would have liked to go on holding it, but she discretely pulled away.

Not certain how to respond after his touch, Erin said, "I enjoyed learning about your youth. Thanks for sharing." She broke eye contact, glanced around the nearly empty room, then down at her wristwatch. "Maybe we ought to be going. I can't believe it's after three."

Jordan grinned. "We haven't talked much about Indian Man."

"What's there to say? Once we agree on a price and where you intend to keep him, that'll be that."

Getting to know Jordan better only perplexed Erin more. No longer was he the ogre she could hate. Just the reverse. She found herself drawn to him, even if she wasn't quite sure of his motives.

"Say, how about a walk on the beach?" he said after he'd paid the bill and they were strolling to their parked cars.

She thought about it. "I've got scads of things to do back at the ranch."

"Just a short one? The weather's perfect."

Erin didn't feel like herself, at all. She wanted to

run along the water's edge and splash and play like a child, forgetting the chores that waited for her. "You talked me into it, but just a short one. Why do I feel like I've been let out of school early?"

He laughed.

Erin followed him in her Jeep down the road and they parked alongside each other in the State Park beach lot.

Jordan got out and opened her car door. "The only way to do this is barefoot," he said, looking down at his shoes.

She grinned. "I haven't gone barefooted in a long time."

He breathed in the clean salt air while they took off their shoes. She rolled up her sleeves to the elbows. Her face glowed.

She's not half as tough as she wants me to think, he told himself.

They walked along the water's foamy brink, scattering sandpipers. The sun cast bronze prisms on the ocean as the waves gently splashed their bare feet. Jordan watched her. She was no Barbie doll. Attractive and petitely built, she apparently loved the open and seemed in her element, passionately interested in everything around her.

"What a lovely day," she said. "Thanks for inviting me. I haven't been here in ages."

He liked the sparkle in her voice. "You're welcome. I'm glad we came."

Her smile warmed him, her face radiant in the sun. The greenish tint of her hazel eyes seemed more vivid than he remembered. He took her hand and they walked up the beach.

A sailboat passed in the distance, seagulls flocking in its wake. The people aboard must be fishing, he thought. The wind transported other sailboats. He turned and caught Erin looking up at him curiously. He smiled.

After a moment, she put on her sunglasses. "Do you come here often?" she asked.

"Wish I could. Like you, it's been a long time."

She bent down and picked up a sand dollar, examined it minutely, then tossed it in the waves. "Do you ever sail?" she asked.

"Not much, but I'd like to more often. Maybe you'd agree to come along one of these days?"

"Oh, I don't know. Things are pretty up in the air for us right now."

He didn't reply, and pushed back a pang of guilt. Did she say that on purpose to get back at him? Somehow, he doubted it. There was a maturity about her, not like some of the self-centered young women he saw at the college. That component in Erin could only come from caring for something bigger than herself.

The thought made him feel even guiltier. Could he really allow the small ranch to be yanked away from the Furys? But if he went up against the trustees' decision too vigorously, it could jeopardize his position.

Just then, a Marine helicopter from nearby Camp Pendleton crept up softly to follow the coastline. As it skittered past the beach, its rotors drowned out their voices, along with the crash of the surf.

Jordan moved closer to Erin, sensing the energy spreading from her. He wanted to reach out, touch her creamy skin, run his fingers along her cheekbone. Could she be aware of these things? She took in everything, from the egret that flew low over the waves, to the tiny sand crabs that buried themselves as soon as the water receded. Yet she didn't seem to notice his profound interest in her.

"Let's sit down over here," he said.

She followed him to a small knoll and they dropped onto the warm, dry sand. He stuck his long legs out in front of him, observing the sand on his bare feet. The tops were beginning to sunburn.

Erin scanned the water. "Maybe we'll see some dolphins or even catch sight of a whale."

"You never know. It's that time of year."

They sat quietly, peacefully absorbing the scene as well as each other. He leaned back, his arms crossed behind his neck. She cupped her knees under her chin and folded her arms around them.

"Being a beachcomber wouldn't be a bad life," he said.

"Or a mermaid."

He turned to face her. "I'd like to see the wind in your hair out there on the water." He motioned toward a boat skimming past.

She instinctively put her hands up and tried to smooth it down, but the breeze was too strong and she gave up, laughing. "My hair must look like a mop about now."

"No, it doesn't. It's beautiful. Makes you look free, without a care in the world."

He hoped he didn't sound like a romantic jerk. Thinking about her, he realized he hadn't felt this relaxed in a long while.

A bank of stratus clouds formed over Santa Catalina Island and a battleship inched along on the horizon.

Children waded in the low surf, their mothers reclining under umbrellas, keeping a watchful eye on them.

Jordan and Erin went on talking, oblivious to time, unfettered by any subject in particular. Listening to her, he realized they had more in common than he thought.

Then Erin glanced toward the west. "Oh, gosh, I think we ought to be starting back," she said, glancing at her watch. "We've been here longer than I realized. It's only a blink away from sundown."

Did he hear a regret in Erin's voice? Musing about her consternation, he put down a hand and rose to his feet, then helped her to rise. He didn't want to leave just yet but knew they must go. She packed up her sunglasses.

The vibrant, lavender and pink brushstrokes of approaching sunset crept across the sky.

"How did it get so late?" he said.

She laughed lightly. "You tell me."

Jordan followed her home, saying he wanted to take a look at Indian Man again. Erin knew it was a ruse but didn't object. The afternoon had been wonderful, and she'd discovered interesting things about him.

They strolled into the darkening stables. Erin switched on an overhead light. The horses shifted and their eyes blinked. Jordan peered over Indian Man's stall gate. The horse came up to them and stuck out his long neck, looking for a treat.

"Yeah, he hasn't developed any spots since I saw him last," Jordan said, teasing. "But I wish I had something to give him. I'll remember next time."

Erin ripped a handful of alfalfa from a bale on the

floor and gave it to Jordan. He handed it over to the horse.

"Want to have something cold to drink?" she asked. "I've got a couple of cans in the office."

"Sure."

They walked the few feet away and she opened the small refrigerator.

"Coke or Sprite?"

"Coke's fine."

She took out the cans and let him open them. "We could sit in the garden for a little while if you want," she said.

"Great idea."

She turned off the stable lightswitch and they sauntered to the garden in the growing twilight. Side by side, they lounged in the glider swing. The garden, fragrant and cool, was a jungle of flowers and vines.

Erin found Jordan easy to talk to, considering the contrast in their education. She wondered if he would rather be discussing Dante or Homer, but that wasn't her thing. She smiled to herself. He obviously knew more about academic life than she ever would yet he never brought up the subject. He placed his arm along the back of the cushion but didn't touch her shoulders. She slowly rocked the swing, feeling remarkably content.

"Tell me more about yourself," he said.

"Didn't you hear enough all afternoon?"

"How about your favorite book. I already know you like Garth Brooks' songs."

"I'd have to think about it."

He grinned. "You must be a Libra. You never answer without giving any question I ask a thought or two, do you?"

Her hand went to her throat and she gave him a long look. "No, I am not a Libra. And my favorite book is a very old novel, *Gone With the Wind.* But I'll bet yours is *War and Peace* or something Dostoyevsky wrote."

He laughed. "I'm not really an intellectual, Erin."

"Well, I'm certainly not. I took animal husbandry in college. I wanted to be a vet."

"Why didn't you go on?"

"Dad needed me."

He didn't comment, and she was glad.

"Don't you get lonely sometimes, with your family being so far away?" she asked.

"Actually, I hadn't thought about it, but I guess I do."

"Didn't you want to be a farmer, too, like your father?"

He nodded. "When I was a kid. But I took a different route."

"I guess not everything turns out the way you expect."

He took a drink. "Mmm."

"So what's it like being a big, important college official making all those decisions?"

He hedged. "The work is rewarding, and it's a step."

"A step to what? You don't sound all that enthused. I thought you'd spiel off all kinds of wonderful things—like power, prestige, a female staff panting after the top man."

He threw his head back and laughed. "You've got it all figured out, have you? Sorry, but it's not like that. In fact, the staff and I often don't see eye to eye. They like the status quo. Then there's the college's trustees. Got to keep them happy. My contract doesn't spell that out in so many words but that's the bottom line in any case."

"Sounds grim."

"Not really. I get some pretty good perks."

She gave him a fixed look, then said impulsively, "Like playing tennis in the middle of the day?"

"That's one of them." His eyes twinkled in the fading light.

"And the step?"

"To a big-name university."

"I see." She looked at him without smiling. "You mentioned your barbecuing expertise. Are you going to invite me over? I'm curious to see where you live."

He didn't blink. "Tomorrow night?"

"No, not tomorrow, but soon."

"The day after?"

Erin sighed heavily, thinking it wasn't really a very good idea. "I shouldn't have said that."

He straightened. "Why?"

"You know."

"Because of the ranch? That's business, Erin. This is you and me we're talking about here."

"I'm afraid I can't separate the two so easily."

He took a deep breath. "I've asked the trustees to reverse their decision. Now we'll just have to see what happens next."

"If you didn't know me, would it be all right to close the ranch?"

He gave a short laugh. "Give me a break, will you? Not renewing your lease wasn't well thought out. I admit it. But it's done. I can only try to change the outcome."

She looked contrite. "Sorry. That was a cheap shot on my part."

"I've made a lot of mistakes in my life, Erin. I'm the one who's sorry."

A measure of intimacy shrouded them with the growing dimness. A chill coming off the ocean a few miles away dampened the air. Erin shivered. She didn't want the evening to end.

"I ought to be getting Dad's supper on the table."

"Yeah, it's about that time." He looked up. "This has to be the world's biggest sky."

She followed his gaze. "It's like glimpsing infinity."

Neither of them made the first move to get up.

"Those stars are beautiful, aren't they?" he went on. "I guess I haven't really looked at them for a long time."

"I have my favorites," she said.

Jordan glanced at her as she looked at the Big Dipper. "Which ones?"

"Those," she said, and pointed a slender finger.

Jordan noticed how lovely she looked, her skin pearl-like in the light of the full moon. He wondered what her lips would feel like if he traced their outline. Then he swallowed hard, bridling his desire. This wasn't the time or place. He wouldn't chance a kiss again, knowing it wasn't fair. Not as long as they were adversaries—business adversaries. Darn! Why had he ever made that cockamamie proposal to the trustees in the first place? This little ranch was an outpost of surging life.

With a calmness he really didn't feel, he said, "Can I see you again soon?"

To his surprise, she didn't hesitate. "Call me."

Jordan badly wanted to kiss her, breathe in the scent of her hair, feel the smoothness of her skin against his cheek. But he kept his emotions in check—not willing to chance Erin taking offense.

Erin turned sideways and peered up at him in the velvety hush.

"You said you're not married, but have you ever been?" she asked.

Her question was blunt and to the point, but that's the kind of person she was. "Close once. And you?"

She threw him a sturdy smile he could barely see now. "I haven't even come near."

He wondered about ol' Stuart. "Seeing someone seriously?"

"No to that one, too. And you?"

He shook his head.

She stared ahead, deep in her own thoughts. A large dog came up to her, sat down, and placed a paw on her lap.

"Lucky's a big ol' dog," she said, cuddling him to her. "I love him to pieces."

Jordan wished he could change places temporarily with the dog.

"He's Dad's dog, really. I'm surprised he's not snoozing beside his chair right now. That means Dad has finished his nap and will be wondering why I'm not in there cooking supper."

He stroked the dog's back and ruffled his ears. "Nice dog."

"I really have to go in," she said wistfully.

Jordan stood and held out his hand to her. She took it. Her small hand felt so fragile, yet there was a strength in the way she clung to his as she rose to her feet. They stared at each other for a moment, as though neither of them knew quite what to do next.

He gave her a stalwart smile, thinking again it would be a perfect time to kiss her. He might think it, but he doubted he'd make any Brownie points with her if he did. She paused, a look of regret in her eyes, and she tilted her face up to him most appealingly. What was a man supposed to do? He took her in his arms and kissed her, good and proper. Her body, at first receptive, tightened and she stepped back from him.

Erin let her breath out in a long sigh, feeling strangely unraveled. She tried to comprehend the emotions running riot inside her. "That was some kiss," she said, not holding back a smile.

"I want you in my life," he said.

"I don't know, Jordan."

"Your kiss has already told me you agree."

He had kissed her, and Erin wanted him to. But she wasn't naive, knowing a gal had to kiss a lot of frogs before finding her prince.

Chapter Five

Erin started for the door but turned back when Jordan said, "I had a great time today." His intimate tone made her smile. The corners of his eyes crinkled as he fixed her with a satisfied grin under the moonlit sky.

Erin tried to make her voice sound calm when she was anything but inside. "Me, too."

He turned away and walked back to where his car was parked. She waited under the porch light until he started to pull away, wondering if he might glance in the rearview mirror as he headed down the dark, rutted road. The wind came up sending whispers through the trees.

When she came inside the living room, Mike's

ruddy cheeks flushed and he tightened his mouth in irritation. The cat draped across his knees.

"Hi, Dad." She leaned over and gave him a kiss on the forehead.

She wanted to share with someone all the emotions stirring inside her but she knew her father wasn't that person. He hated Jordan Archer and everything he stood for.

His eyes narrowed and a muscle in his jaw tightened. "Why did you want to go off and have lunch with that man? And you've been gone all afternoon."

She spread her hands in mild frustration. "We talked mostly business."

"That man's a burr under my saddle, girl. We're in a mess, thanks to him, and you just remember that. Sometimes you sure can be naive and sentimental, just like your ma. Don't let him hoodwink you now, hear?"

She lifted a shoulder dismissively. "I wasn't born under a turnip truck."

Her father usually laughed at her old clichés but his mouth didn't turn up. He crammed his big fists into his pockets and stretched in the chair. The cat jumped down, scowling, and wandered away.

"I'll fix supper. Sorry it's so late."

Erin could feel his stern, parental gaze on her back as she walked out of the room. Maybe he was right. Was she being taken in, and making a fool of herself in the process? Her doubts surged. She moved aimlessly around the kitchen, opening the refrigerator and running water over a head of lettuce. Then she grasped the smooth top of the chair and sat down, burying her face in her hands. What had she done? She had practically melted into the enemy camp's arms like a traitor! Her anxiety broke apart and she came close to shedding a tear. Feeling sorry for herself wasn't something she gave in to easily. She rested her chin in a palm, elbow on the table, and ran her tongue across her lips, telling herself she wouldn't be so stupid the next time she saw Jordan. But still, his kiss had been so tender.

The following morning's horseback riding session went well and Erin helped young Josh out of the saddle. He was beaming. His mother, Sarah, took off his helmet and brushed out a tangle with her fingers. Her long, dark hair shimmered down her back. She gave it a swish that sent it cascading around her shoulders.

"Can we come again next week?" he asked in a rush.

Josh's voice was high, childlike, but in no time it would change, Erin thought as she nodded. "Sure. Same time, same channel."

He laughed, giving her a happy face, and hobbled off to talk to some of the other children. Erin tied the pony's reins to a hitching post.

"How was the lunch date with Mister Handsome?" Sarah asked. Her lips turned up in a grin.

"It wasn't a date," Erin chided her friend.

"Then what do you call it?"

"Business. He wants to buy the thoroughbred. Remember, I told you all about it?"

"Uh-huh, if you say so." Sarah gave a slight shrug. "Seriously, though, you ought to admit you like him. He's quite a fox."

"You're going too fast, reading all kinds of things

into something that isn't there." Erin steepled her fingers, distracted.

"C'mon. This is me."

Erin sighed. "Actually, he wasn't hard to talk to, after I got over being sort of nervous around him."

"And?"

"What can I say? I had a good time."

"When are you going to see him again?"

"Aren't you just full of questions? Seriously, I don't think I should. The ranch and all. Where's my loyalty, anyway? Certainly not to Jordan Archer."

Sarah glanced over Erin's shoulder. "Speak of the devil, here he comes."

Erin heard the sound of a car engine speeding up the drive and turned to see Jordan's BMW approaching. "Oh, my!" she said.

Sarah grinned, and grasped her hands behind her back.

When Jordan stopped at the ranch, Erin was chatting with an attractive, dark-haired woman he vaguely remembered meeting somewhere. He joined them and Erin introduced him to Sarah Whitefeather. They chatted for a few minutes about once meeting at the mission, then Sarah and her son left.

Erin seemed cool, indifferent, saying she was awfully busy.

He followed her into the stables, feeling his own irritation growing inside him. "Look, I'm really trying here," he said. "And I'm not such a bad person, Erin. Why, I was even a Boy Scout." His attempt at humor didn't work, so he asked her flat out, "How come you're giving me this silent treatment?"

Erin gave Jordan a weak smile. "I'm not, but you must understand there's a lot to do around here."

Dressed in cutoffs that showed off her shapely legs, and a tank top, she took Indian Man out of the stall, and began to groom the horse with a currycomb. He admired her economy of motion as she worked. He could see they weren't going to be on the same track they'd been on the day before. Managing a bland smile, he puzzled over the reason. Women and their mystery element! But then, maybe that's what attracted men, he thought ruefully.

Still, he had to admit, Erin Fury wasn't like most women he knew. He liked her pluck and tenacity, but he didn't understand this standoffishness. And for a moment he felt awkward, wondering at himself—he, the college president who was usually so sure of everything.

"So, how are things going?" Erin asked, detached. Not looking at Jordan, she combed out the horse's long mane, standing on her toes.

"I've had better days."

She didn't reply, just reached up high to brush between the bay's ears.

"Why do I feel I've said something wrong?" he asked.

She looked him square in the eyes. "It's *done* something wrong—not said something."

"Oh, I see. We're back to the lease."

"Exactly."

Jordan felt like he was in freefall. This was a woman with fire in her belly. He had to respect her for that, like it or not. But he didn't have to like the ire aimed at him, especially after yesterday. One part of him wanted to lash out angrily, defend himself, but another part felt her sadness, and the ache in his gut grew stronger when he saw the look on her face.

"You have every right to be angry," he said. "I'm responsible for this whole thing, and I wish I could change it. But my feelings for you are quite separate."

He could see her mood lighten. "Sorry," she said. "I didn't mean to rub it in."

Watching her, he remembered every word she had uttered the day before, and how she had looked at him after he subdued Indian Man in the canyon.

Erin put the comb on a shelf and led the horse outside. She brushed away a strand of mane that whipped up against the horse's face in the breeze. Jordan followed, thinking she lived in a different world from his.

When Erin opened the gate and loosed the horse in the pasture with other horses browsing idly together, she turned back to Jordan and smiled.

"Indian Man doesn't have any serious problems," she said, totally changing the subject. "If you notice, when he walks head-on, he doesn't walk wide, which sometimes indicates something amiss."

He noticed the dewy moisture on her forehead. "You're very knowledgeable about horses, Erin."

She hesitated. "I enjoyed being with you yesterday, but I'm not ready to write an epitaph for our enterprise here, not just because of it."

He swallowed hard. "Is that what you thought—I was trying to smooth things over until the hatchet falls? That simply isn't true."

He didn't want to tell her just how much he cared about her, not until he was able to undue what he'd done. But darn it, he did care, and a lot more than he wanted to admit even to himself.

She stared at him. "In the beginning, I thought you didn't care a nickel what happened here. I was determined I wouldn't give you the satisfaction of seeing my frayed nerves. But now I don't know whether you're for real or not. I want to think you are."

Jordan gave her a thin smile. "I don't want you to lose the ranch, Erin, and I'm trying my best to influence the trustees. What can I say? At least give me a chance."

A day would come when he'd have to stand up and be counted.

Erin didn't speak for a few moments. It nearly drove him out of his mind. Then she exhaled a deep breath. "I guess we'll just have to wait until the meeting, then."

Her dismissal hurt but he veiled his eyes as best he could, and brushed at a fly. "I'll be in touch."

The telephone rang. Erin went to answer it. He stood there, waiting for her to come back, asking himself why he didn't leave.

She came out of the stables, an excitement on her face. He sensed it wasn't because of him.

"I've got to find Dad. We've been called over to the Aliso Viejo Company to herd the last of their cattle to the holding pens. They're shipping them out to Montana. More of your progress," she said with a snide twist to her mouth. "They'll be building more tracts."

"When are you going?"

"In the morning. Why, do you want to come

along?" She said it playfully, as though she expected him to decline.

"Why not? I've got a horse now."

The business of the horse had been settled the night before in a call from Erin.

"You're kidding? You'd ride Indian Man to do that kind of work? He's not a cutting horse."

"So be it. We'll learn together."

"Don't you have to work?"

"I have more than a few days coming."

"Be here at dawn, sharp. We won't wait if you oversleep."

He took out his wallet and handed her the check for Indian Man. She smiled, then turned and hurried toward the house, He stood there a moment, admiring the sight before replacing his wallet.

Chapter Six

Jordan barely made it by dawn the following morning. Yawning, he saddled Indian Man and mounted. The horse pranced, friskier than Jordan had ever seen him. Jim O'Toole was already there with the chuckwagon, his kitchen on wheels.

"Those steers see that horse and they'll line up for a race," Mike Fury said, laughing at Jordan's expense.

Jordan smiled. "He'll do just fine."

Erin was the last to mount, checking this and that. They headed out, moving north. The sun was well up when they reached the spreading Aliso Viejo and began the dusty, tiring work of rounding up the sparsely grouped steers.

If he hadn't known it, Jordan wouldn't have believed they were in Orange County. Cactus bloomed in the back country. The acrid scent of mesquite and sage made him feel nostalgic for a simpler way of life, even though the saddle was already getting hard on his posterior.

They circled around, down one draw after another, as the herd gradually increased. The cattle bawled. Other cowboys had joined them. After awhile, they stopped for lunch. Erin took her aluminum plate and cup and found a place to sit down in the shade of a lone oak tree. Her face was covered with a fine silt of dust, making her eyes look even bigger. The cowboy hat atop her thick curls had dirt embedded in its straw, probably sifting down on the crown of her head, Jordan thought. But she seemed not to notice or care. This was a job to be done and Erin Fury knew how to do that very well.

Jordan took off his own hat and hit it against his thigh, watching the dust swirl. He picked up his food from O'Toole and joined Erin. The cattle hardly moved in the noonday sun, tranquil as old hound dogs.

He groaned when he sat down.

"Long morning, huh?" she said with a touch of sympathy. "It must be great to have a day job you can just take off from anytime the mood moves you."

"I rescheduled my appointments. Are you giving me an A or an F, teacher?"

"That's up to you. But thanks for coming along. It would have been doubly hard with just Dad, Stu, and this handful of guys."

Hal, a quiet man, was one of the volunteers who Jordan had seen a time or two at the ranch. He and Stuart came up and sat down by Erin, disappointing Jordan.

"How are things going?" Jordan asked Stuart.

"Not bad."

Then Stuart turned his attention to Erin and they started talking about things that didn't concern Jordan, like how much feed Stuart needed to pick up at the feed store.

Jordan finished eating and stood up, trying to think of something to bring Erin's attention back to him. He could talk about Indian Man. But that might not be such a good idea. The gelding wasn't too interested in herding cattle, although he seemed to like dashing for them when they tried to break away.

He took his plate back to the chuckwagon. Mike and Jim had their heads together in conversation. Jim lounged up against the wagon, smoking a pipe. "We should be able to get the steers to those holding pens by nightfall," Mike said. He looked up at the sun and shaded his eyes. "We better get moving."

"I'll put things away now and secure them," Jim said, then bellowed to the others, "Okay, folks, bring me your plates."

Shortly after, everyone mounted and the cattle moved in a northern direction. The break had done Jordan good. He was enjoying himself. It was every man's dream. The Old West come to life.

He thought of the western books and movies he'd seen of men on cattle drives, challenged by outlaws and the elements. Daydreaming, he nearly fell asleep in the saddle. He pictured himself as Sam Shepard, the gun-slinger who faced down bad guys in the television mini series "Purgatory"—the good and the bad playing out against each other. Then there were Billy Crystal and Jack Palance in their humor-filled cattle drive movie.

Jordan opened his eyes. The scattered clouds had turned ominously thick and bullet gray. Thunder rolled across the terrain, followed by a sharp clap of lightning. Indian Man nearly jumped out from under him but he managed to quiet the horse. They were passing a high mesa when their trail riding was disrupted by raindrops and jittery steers.

"We'll gather the cattle closer together," Erin called to Jordan and the others. "Move them in."

They began to swing the cattle into a bunch. Rain trickled off Jordan's hat and down his back, making him feel clammy. The temperature dropped.

"Darn it, who said anything about inclement weather," he muttered.

Then the rain came down in a deluge. They slogged on. He hoped it was only a cloudburst. They all hunched over in the saddles, their hats pulled low, as the ride turned messy. The parched earth soaked up the moisture and the adobe beneath it turned slippery.

Another peal of thunder boomed around their ears and lightning sparked in the sky. The horses slipped and slid in places, making traveling treacherous and slow. Jordan hunkered down, as the thought of getting fried like a slice of bacon by a bolt of lightning crossed his mind.

Then the biggest clap of thunder he'd ever heard assaulted him, raising the hairs on his arms. The nervous steers stamped and took off at a clumsy run.

Mike yelled, "Head them off. There's a deep gully coming up."

Jordan let Indian Man stretch out in a gallop. He saw Erin take off too on Angel Face. Just as they were funneling the herd into manageable control, the mare slipped and Erin went flying. Horrified, Jordan acted on instinct before the steers could trample her. He jumped off his horse and pulled her back to safety.

"You all right, Erin?" he demanded. She had the wind knocked out of her. He heard her take a breath and his heart turned over.

"Yeah. Help me back on my horse. We don't have a minute to waste."

"Let me look at you first. You may be hurt and not even know it."

"Jordan, for Pete's sake. This isn't the first time I've been thrown. Come on now. Grab Angel Face's reins before she takes off."

Grumbling, he reluctantly did as she said. Mud caked Erin's shoulder where she'd landed on her side. He helped her mount, then swung into the saddle. She didn't even wait for him but took off like a banshee, mud flying from the horse's hooves. He let Indian Man follow, praying the horse wouldn't break a leg. With the others assisting, they turned the steers in another direction.

When it was over, the rain stopped. They moved the cattle forward until they reached the holding pens and guided them inside. A huge cattle truck stood waiting. Several men, wearing slickers, began leading the steers along a shoot into the bowels of the truck. Mike and Erin talked with the men. The head of the group thanked them. With business concluded, Jordan glanced up at the western sky. The sun peeked through the clouds as though blowing them away on either side. In spite of everything, the party of riders had made good time.

Mike took off his hat and waved it forward. "Let's go home, folks. Job well done."

Jordan could have sworn Mike was looking right at him as dusk turned the land to a tarnished gold.

Two days later, Jordan called Erin. Her voice sounded airy at first, but as soon as he gave his name, it turned strained, business-like.

"Hi," she said.

"What are you doing?" he asked.

"The usual."

"I've missed you."

She sighed. "Jordan, I don't think we're right for each other."

"You sound awfully sure."

"Why did you call? Did you find out something?" she asked, changing the subject.

He hated disappointing her. "I got you a ninety-day extension. After that, I can't promise anything. It's wait and see time, I'm afraid."

He could almost hear the long, deep sigh on the other end. He should have put a better spin on it. But how? He closed his eyes, then opened them wide, willing her to speak.

"Thanks, Jordan. At least that gives us some breathing space."

"Sometimes I think I'll wake up and this will all have blown over, brightening the future for you and your father," he said in a wishful tone.

"That sounds like one of my dreams. Actually, I always thought I could alter the course of things just by sheer will. Now I'm about as unsure of myself as I can be." Her voice sounded so down.

"None of us likes to be in that position, I know. Just hold on for awhile," he said, wanting to comfort her.

"Easy for you to say."

He stared moodily out the large expanse of windows in his office. He was used to making things happen. Why couldn't he do it now?

"I'll keep in touch," he said, then replaced the receiver in its cradle.

The following Saturday Jordan showed up at the Fury ranch. Erin saw him walking toward her, tall, muscular and tawny. He wasn't wearing one of his pressed suits or polished Wingtips, but well-worn Wranglers and a faded blue shirt.

"I'm here to volunteer," he announced to a surprised Erin. "You name it. I'll do just about anything."

She chuckled. "See that manure pile." She slanted a glance behind her. "It needs to go on the back of the pickup, then hauled to the dump. Can you do that?"

"Let's say it wasn't what I had in mind, but sure, I'll do it."

She looked down. "It's a good thing you wore old boots."

"Yeah, I can see that. I dug these out of storage."

A car pulled into the yard, followed by several more, and children piled out, laughing and talking excitedly.

"I'll be giving lessons all morning," she told him. "If you need anything, why, don't hesitate to call me."

Jordan caught the mischievous look in her eyes and vowed he'd do a fine job, even if it killed him. Stuart was washing down a horse near the stable entrance, one eye peeled on the two of them. Jordan nodded to him. Just how close was Erin to the man? Certainly Stuart put in an inordinate amount of time volunteering.

Erin went off to see to the children. Jordan turned and sauntered over to take a look at Indian Man. He was proud of how the horse handled himself during the roundup. Jordan caught the earthy smell of the saddled horses as he passed them.

Clean, coarse straw had been scattered on the floor of Indian Man's stall. Jordan knew he really ought to be coming over every morning and tending to the horse's needs himself before going to his office, like other owners did.

Jordan ended up staying through the afternoon. When he came back from the dump, he hosed off the truck-bed. Then he began grooming his horse, humming tunelessly to himself. Stuart was still there, polishing leather saddles to a sheen. Cushy job, Jordan thought enviously. He caught the man eyeing him, and the look wasn't too friendly. Stuart had a giant crush on Erin. That was a given. What man wouldn't?

When everyone left and the day drew to a close, Erin finally took notice of Jordan. He was airing saddle blankets.

She smiled. "Thanks for helping out today. Looks like you did a good job."

He knew he must stink to high heaven, and since he hadn't shaved that morning, he probably looked like a real cowhand. "I think you're welcome, but I'll let you know after I pay a visit to a chiropractor."

She chuckled. A pigeon's soft fluttering wings soared overhead and it landed in a tree, making cooing sounds in its throat. He took Erin's hand lightly in his soiled one.

"Let me look at your face," he said with a curious gaze, half serious, half amused.

"Oh, stop," she said, pulling her hand away with a twinkle in her eye.

"You have an intoxicating smile, but your nose has a smudge of dirt on the tip, ma'am."

"Quit your teasing."

"Let your heart hear what I'm trying to say, Erin."

"More poetry? I don't believe a word you're saying."

"I haven't said it yet."

"Well, go on then."

"I'm weak with starvation. How about a crust of bread, or better still, I'll take you out after I wash this ton of dirt off."

"You mean you didn't take time to have lunch?"

"How could I? You gave me too many chores to do."

"Okay, I'll take pity on you. You can stay for dinner if you wash up, including your boots. But don't expect anything gourmet."

Jordan cleaned himself as best he could in the stables. Erin and Mike were already in the house. He knocked and she let him in. He glanced around at the well-cared for, worn furniture. A handmade sampler quilt was neatly folded on the back of the sofa. A cuckoo clock hung over the fireplace mantle. Mike said hi without enthusiasm, holding a coffee mug clamped tight in a big fist.

"Take a seat," he said, slanting his eyes at the

drooping leather sofa. The dog thumped his tail beside him as he eased himself back into an overstuffed chair by the unlit fireplace. "Coffee?"

"I'll wait," Jordan said. He picked up a quarterhorse magazine off the coffee table and thumbed through it, pointing out a picture of a dapple gray horse to Mike. The older man nodded approval.

Erin came back. She'd put on clean jeans and a sweatshirt with a picture of a wagon with bright flowers spilling over the sides.

"Supper's ready, you two," she said.

They rose in unison. When Mike walked ahead of him, Jordan noticed he had a limp. Erin looked lovely, her movements quick and fluid as she moved around the kitchen.

"You sit there." She indicated a chair on the right. Her father took a seat at the head of the table.

Erin served the meal family style. Jordan liked sitting down to a home cooked dinner like his mom used to make, even if Erin's father hadn't warmed up to him yet.

Jordan waited for Mike to pick up his fork before he began. Erin appeared a trifle nervous, glancing from her father to him, then down to her plate. She sat stiffly in the chair. Then they both reached for a roll in the basket and smiled self-consciously when their fingers touched. Jordan took a bite of roast beef and added a dollop of horseradish-laced sour cream.

"This is delicious," he said between bites.

Erin smiled. "Thanks."

Mike continued to eat, watching Jordan from across the table, his mouth set disapprovingly. "So you bought Indian Man?" he said, breaking his silence. He picked up the mug and gulped down coffee.

Jordan couldn't help but feel the tension in the room. Obviously Erin's father didn't like having him there. He was still surprised Erin had asked him to stay in the first place. "Yes. I think he and I mix well."

"Humph." he said.

Jordan searched for something appropriate to say. "I understand you've got a mare who's about to foal."

"Stu's taken the horse off our hands. Maybe she'll foal in the next week," Mike replied. "He'll be keeping an eye on her udder."

Erin explained. "That's how you can tell when the mare's ready."

Jordan nodded. It was news to him. Her father seemed more approachable when the topic was horses, so he milked it. "I understand a horse is one year older on New Years Day, no matter when it's born."

"That's what the breeders of thoroughbreds say," Mike conceded.

"Seems odd."

Mike didn't say anything else, and dinner went on rather strained.

When the meal was over, Erin started clearing the table. Jordan lent a hand. Her father left them and wandered off to the living room, his dog following like a trusting friend. Jordan suggested he and Erin take a walk after they'd washed the dishes and put them away.

"The evenings have warmed considerably," she said, even though she grabbed a sweater off a hook by the kitchen door when they stepped outside.

He heard a horse nicker softly in the stillness.

"Horses have a language of their own," she said, reading his thoughts. "Ever heard of Monty Roberts?"

"Don't people call him the Horse Whisperer, or something like that?"

"Yeah. He's just great. Dad went to one of his seminars once. Ever since, we've tried to follow his model of working with horses who've had a rough past. Works fine."

These are solid people, Jordan thought. They gave so much of themselves and they certainly deserved better than what they were about to get.

Together, not touching, Erin and Jordan fell into step and headed toward the orange grove.

"Smell those blossoms," she said. "They're heavenly. When my dad was a boy this whole valley was thick with these groves. How things have changed."

"I would like to have seen it then," Jordan said.

A cloudy veil whispered across the moon, temporarily making things darker, until it passed on. She hoped it obscured the look that might have been on her face as well.

"You must have loved school," she said in a playful tone. "What were you like in college? Studious? Your nose stuck in books all the time?"

"Hardly."

"No? I bet you charmed all the girls and were voted most likely to succeed."

He grinned. "Neither. You've got me all wrong. Actually, I got in to college on a baseball scholarship."

"You're pulling my leg."

"Scouts honor." He raised a hand with the two-finger salute. "I didn't really get interested in academics until graduate school."

"You gave up baseball then?"

"Had to, although it was a tough decision."

"And the Ph.D.?"

"Seemed like the right thing to do. A guy's got to work at something to get ahead."

"I'm impressed."

"You needn't be." Yet hearing her say the words gave Jordan a lift.

"You know, our worlds are as different as night and day, you in your ivory tower and me mucking out stalls."

He laughed, not sure of what she was driving at. "Why do you say that? Seems like those roles were reversed today."

Her chuckle seemed genuine, though tinged with embarrassment. "Well, I never finished college. You're a college president. I wear jeans. You're used to women who wear linen, and silk, and expensive perfumes. You probably like to order capons in some fancy restaurant. I like Big Mac hamburgers."

He shook his head and reached out, giving her a hug before he thought about it. She didn't appear disgruntled.

"You're all wrong," he said.

They reached the orange grove, with its squat, well manicured trees. Erin gave a slight cough and moved out of his range. The magnificent scent of orange blossoms made him almost dizzy.

He gathered his thoughts. "You never talk much about yourself, and now you're telling me how different we are," he said. "Somehow, our conversations always get back to me."

"My life wouldn't interest you. I did win a barrel

race once when I was sixteen. Got a blue ribbon. Does that make an impression on you?" She smiled.

"*You* impress me," he said.

Their eyes locked.

She turned away, wiping all emotion from her face. He wished he could put into words what he felt without sounding stupid, but those fine words wouldn't come.

The moonlight teased her hair, giving it a golden luminescent quality, and her eyes softened as they walked on slowly, side by side. He couldn't imagine wanting to be anywhere else or with anyone else. And he wished she'd let him know by a hint or gesture if she felt the same way.

They made a full circle and headed back to the garden. He turned to face her. She stopped, watching him with a curious glint. His need to hold her surged like a summer storm inside him. He held out his arms, his eyes pleading, and to his surprise, she glided into them and he enfolded her. His breath quickened and his heart skipped when he caught the sweet scent of her. The warmth of her body through her clothing melded with his and he felt her heartbeat beneath his own. His lips grazed her throat. In the next moment, he bent his head, found her yielding lips and covered them gently with his own.

Pulling back briefly to check her expression for a sign of acceptance, he kissed her again, hungrily. He buried his fingers in her thick hair as her lips parted, and she returned his kiss.

With arms wrapped around each other as though fearful of being separated, they stood there, oblivious to time.

When Erin finally pulled back, Jordan held her loosely. "It's not ever going to be the same for us, Erin. You must realize it, too."

"What now?" she said in a small voice.

"You know what."

"But how can we go on seeing each other—build a relationship? There's the matter of the ranch. Dad's beside himself with anxiety. He would never approve." She sighed wistfully. "Don't you see? Our differences are insurmountable."

He gave her a smile from the heart. "This need we share for each other is something, isn't it? But our caring is more important than all the rest. Admit it in your soul."

She didn't reply. A moonbeam glittered a silver streak across her face, making her look otherworldly for an instant. He stood transfixed, stroking her hair back gently.

"Though we may be opposites, some force has brought us together for a reason and you can't fight it anymore than I can," he said soothingly.

Still, she didn't speak.

"Listen to me, Erin. Something profound has happened here tonight, and I don't want it to get lost in all the other confusion."

He could tell she was struggling with her feelings by the slight tremble of her body.

Then she said sadly, "In my heart, I know you're right. But there's the other thing. I can't just forget about what's going to happen to my dad and me, and the children and the horses."

The miserable look on her face made his throat tighten.

"I wish to God I could wave a magic wand and make it all go away, but I can't. You know I'll keep trying my best, though," he said, "no matter what it takes."

Erin sighed deeply. She wanted to believe him. Yet, like trying to control a team of wild horses, she understood that having a relationship with him would only add to the conflict. But when he took her hand, drawing her to him again, she didn't have the fortitude to pull away. She laid her face against his chest. "I can't make any rational decisions when you hold me in your arms like this," she murmured.

Jordan's lips whispered across the crown of her head. She wanted to reach up and bring his mouth to hers, but held back.

"I do care for you," she cried softly. "But all these things are eating me up."

"I care so much about you that it scares me," he said in a husky voice.

Then it hit him like a thunderbolt, and for several seconds he couldn't think of anything to say. He was in love with Erin Fury. He, the consummate bachelor. Why didn't he just come out and tell her, for heaven's sake?

The tenderness in his tone made Erin want to weep as he went on speaking low, a warm breath away from her ear.

"Plain and simple, I think I'm falling in love with you, Erin."

Did she hear right or was it only the sighing of the trees in the soft breeze? She dared not respond, but clung to him, burying her face in the curve of his neck.

Chapter Seven

That night, Erin lay awake for hours, her thoughts roiling. Jordan had said he was in love with her. But what did he really mean to her? Their relationship had accelerated like a roller coaster, moving too fast.

She struggled with the pillows, finally tossing them off the bed into a heap. Even with all the questions she'd put to him, she knew very little about Jordan Archer. Should she trust him? He could be leading her to think they might have a chance to change the board's mind, and know full well they had no intention of doing so. But what would be his motive? Well, she wasn't about to leave anything to chance. That's not the way the Furys did things.

Even though Erin admitted she cared for Jordan, she knew she'd have to put personal feelings aside until the matter of the ranch was finally resolved. She owed it to her father and to the children.

The next day, Erin sat at her desk working on plans for the coming chuckwagon cookout and barn dance. Jordan called. She recognized his voice immediately. Flustered, she dropped the pencil on the floor.

"I miss you," he said. "How am I going to get any work accomplished if you're on my mind all the time?"

She was glad he couldn't see the flush on her face. "Delegate. You've got a secretary, don't you?"

"I like hearing your voice. It's so melodious. Can you get away for lunch today?"

"I'm too busy," she said, teasing, "and I don't have a secretary. But if an extra volunteer came around, that would be nice."

"Wish I could help out but duty calls. Maybe I'll send over my secretary. She's darned efficient."

"No, thanks. She's got too much starch in her bustle for this place."

His voice turned serious. "Can we go somewhere tonight? Maybe take in a movie?"

She hesitated. "Jordan, I don't know if that's such a good idea. I've been thinking. You know, about what you said. We ought to . . ."

"C'mon, Erin. You know that's not true."

"I can't think about our having any kind of relationship until the ranch issue is settled," she rushed on before he could interrupt her again.

Jordan was silent for a moment. She knew she'd hurt him and her heart ached.

He cleared his throat. "I'm going away for a few days," he said. "I was hoping to see you first."

"Oh?" Her heart sped up even while she tried to sound composed. "You didn't mention it last night. Business or pleasure? Miami Beach or New York City?"

Her attempt at humor failed.

"Sacramento," he said flatly. "I'm going to an educational conference. But I'll be back in plenty of time for the board meeting."

"Well then, I'll see you when you get back."

She missed him already.

"Erin?"

"Yes?" She wanted him to go on talking.

"Take care of yourself."

She bit her lip. "You too."

"Yeah. So long."

"Bye."

Why did life have to be so complicated, she asked herself. But in her heart, she knew she was doing the right thing. She couldn't just drop everything every time Jordan Archer called, even though she was sorely tempted.

Briefcase in hand, Jordan hurried along the marble floors and arched ceilings of the jet-age John Wayne Airport to his departure gate. His mind wasn't on the conference or the paper he'd so painstakingly drawn up. It was on Erin Fury and her problems, now his problems as well. Surely he could come up with a logical answer to bring this ranch thing to a satisfactory conclusion. He had even spoken with the college's attorney, and received only a negative response.

* * *

Erin arrived back at the house after having met with the veterinarian about one of the horses who had colic. She jumped in the shower, anxious to make a favorable impression on the trustees at the meeting. Her father had taught her to grapple with life, take it on, tackle it, and not be afraid to take a risk. Well, she couldn't be any more eager to face these people than now.

Jordan had left a message, saying he was back from Sacramento and would see her there. Even with her confidence high, a trickle of nerves slid down her spine. She pulled clothes out of the closet, looking for just the right thing to wear. Jeans she had plenty of, but few things suitable for the meeting.

When the phone rang, she picked it up, not welcoming the distraction. "Hello. Fury Ranch."

"Glad I caught you, Erin," a vaguely familiar voice said. "It's Travis, the dispatcher at the sheriff's office. Seems a horse wandered off up on the Ortega and is stuck in an arroyo. Can't get the poor thing out. Every time one of our guys tries to get near, the horse starts kicking and bucking. Probably scared out of its feedbag. A hiker heard him screeching and went to investigate. The sheriff wondered if you'd help out."

What about the meeting? They were practically on their way. Yet Erin couldn't refuse to help. Down deep, she knew a horse's life came first.

With only a moment's hesitation, she said, "Give me the details. We'll be there." Then she hung up and rang Jordan. No answer. Darn! Leaving a hurried message of apology, she quickened her pace to find her father.

They sped down the highway toward the outskirts of the Cleveland National Forest as fast as they dared with the horse trailer on the back. She hardly noticed the opulence of the sagebrush-covered landscape.

Locating the property wasn't too difficult. Familiar with the area, her father pulled off the road at the fork and yanked the parking brake. A sheriff's SUV drew alongside. Her father got out and pulled his sweat-stained Stetson down low over his eyes, shielding his face from the late afternoon sun.

"You brought a trailer. Good," the deputy said.

"When we get the dang horse out, we can't leave it stranded here, now can we?"

The deputy nodded, tipping his hat.

Erin knew her father had already forgotten about the board meeting, his attention focused on the horse. He could be a rascal at times but he had a heart of gold.

She turned to the deputy, recognizing him. "Has the owner come looking for the horse?"

"Not yet. We phoned two ranchers who live close by, thinking it might be theirs. Neither of them was home. We left messages. The dispatcher is calling around."

The officers helped haul equipment out of the trailer. Then the little group made their way over uneven, gopher hole pocked ground to the forsaken horse.

"A sorry sight," her father muttered after taking a look. Perspiration popped out on his forehead. "We've got our work cut out for us."

The horse's panicked screams and stamping hooves made Erin's heart wrench. She'd seen horses kill themselves thrashing around in fear. This wasn't going to be easy. The two deputies stood watching, waiting to assist in any way they could.

"Glad you made it, Mike," the taller deputy, Todd Elder, said.

Todd went to high school with Erin and he'd played on the varsity football team. She had even dated him a couple of times. He gave her a familiar smile.

"How long has the horse been down there, do you think?" she asked him.

"Could be hours. No one knows for sure. We've sent for a crane."

"Will it be here soon?"

"I hope so. The electric company agreed to donate it."

The situation didn't sound good. Erin's stomach did a flip-flop. There wasn't time for more conversation. "I hope this horse has a guardian angel," she said.

Todd nodded. "Without you and your dad, this horse would be carrion meat by dawn."

Erin grimaced and turned to her father. "Dad, you stay up here. It doesn't look like there's much room down there."

"Now come on, girl. You're not getting down in that hole by yourself," he huffed, rubbing the underside of his chin with his thumbnail. "There could be a cave-in from the looks of it."

"It's the only way. If I'm lucky, I should have the sling fastened under his belly by the time the crane gets here."

Head snapping forward like a turtle's, he finally gave in, mumbling to himself about her having her way.

Erin started down the side of the steep arroyo, praying she wouldn't meet up with a rattlesnake in the scrub brush. Then someone called her name. She turned to look up.

Jordan, dressed in an expensive suit, stood at the rim of the arroyo. "Just what do you think you're doing?"

"I'm about to drag this canvas sling down to the bottom. What did you think I was doing?"

"Oh, no you're not!"

She chuckled. "What's all this? We're wasting precious time."

His eyes turned to steel. "You're not going down there."

"Jordan, really." She looked amused, and turned to go.

He yanked off his suitcoat and tossed it on the ground. Then he reached down and grabbed the sling from her. Tossing the heavy thing over his shoulder, he jumped over the side of the arroyo like Superman. Erin stood there, stunned, lost her footing and plopped on her bottom.

The horse, a sturdy gelding, tossed his head in agitation and shuddered. Jordan kept his arms close to his sides, grateful the gelding hadn't kicked him in the teeth. The horse fidgeted nervously, his dark brown eyes blazing fear. His powerful hooves could rear back and strike out at any time. Jordan proceeded with caution. Loose dirt and small rocks littered the floor of the arroyo.

"Take it easy, boy," he murmured, assessing the animal. Apparently, no broken legs. "I'll get you out of this just as fast as I can or my name's not Jordan Archer."

The splendid creature sniffed the air and made a guttural sound low in its throat as Jordan began the risky process of positioning him into the sling. Several people gathered above, but he hadn't heard the crane arrive.

A man leaned over the side of the arroyo. "I'm Web Jones," he called. "That's my horse. Need a hand?" The glare of the late afternoon sun obscured his features.

"Just a little luck," Jordan replied as he worked. He glanced down at his trousers and groaned at the dirt encrusted on the knees where he'd landed in a sprawl. His best suit. And the horse had stepped on one of his shoes, scarring the top, as well as painfully grinding Jordan's toes into the ground.

The horse's ears pricked forward at the sound of the man's voice. He whinnied and made an attempt to scramble up the side of the arroyo. Jordan threw his arms around the horse's neck. "Whoa!"

"You okay down there?" Erin called.

He liked the tremor in her voice. "Yeah. Is the crane here?"

"It's just coming up now."

"Thank the dear Lord."

The air in the arroyo grew hotter while thick clouds of dust spiraled upward until he could taste it. The walls seemed too close. He said a prayer and finally got the canvas fastened under the panicky gelding.

The crane pulled the horse to safety. Jordan got the heck out of there.

Erin hugged him. "You gave me quite a scare," she said.

Her hug felt good. "Worried about the horse, huh?"

"And you." She chuckled.

The gelding looked a little wobbly. The owner and deputies unfastened the sling. Mike Fury came over and shook Jordan's hand. Rivulets of sweat created a path down Jordan's face. Erin took a tissue from her pocket and wiped his eyes, making a worse mess.

"We'd better get out of here now," she said. "Come back to the ranch with us, Jordan." She had his suit-coat across her arm.

He took the coat and threw it over a shoulder, not caring what happened to his suit now. The horse was safe. Erin was happy. And all was fine with the world.

The other men patted him on the back and congratulated him on what he had managed to accomplish. The horse's owner couldn't give him enough praise. Jordan felt sort of noble now that it was all over. And sore.

Erin wet her lips. "You could have been hurt," she said with obvious concern.

"And you couldn't?"

"That's different."

Oh?"

She laughed, exasperated. "You're impossible, but thanks just the same."

He understood why she couldn't let go of her exasperation. It came from the adrenaline rush. And maybe just a little affection for him.

As they started to walked away, Erin said, "You're a big hero now, Jordan."

He grinned. "Not really. I just couldn't see you going down there."

The owner stopped them. "What do I owe you?"

"Make a contribution to the Fury Ranch's riding program," Jordan said.

The man replied, "Gladly."

They walked on. Jordan was tremendously relieved now that it was all over. Sunlight skipped across the wings of a dragonfly. The trees smelled like perfume.

When they reached her father's pickup, he asked Erin, "Will you go with me to the Swallows Day Parade tomorrow?"

"Sure. Dad will be riding his horse in it."

"Great. And don't be concerned about that board meeting. It's been rescheduled."

She smiled warmly and leaned up to kiss his dirty cheek. "Thanks, Jordan." Looking over her shoulder toward the arroyo, she added, "Thanks again for rescuing the horse."

He swallowed hard.

When he picked Erin up the next day, Jordan complimented her on her clothes—a bright blue plaid western shirt and new jeans that fit like a glove.

"I'm sorry about having to bug-out on the meeting. It means a lot to me and my dad, your rescheduling it to another time. Don't think we didn't feel awful about it. Just tell me when. We'll be there. You understand we had no alternative."

"Sure."

She gave him a speculative look. "How did you know where we would be yesterday?"

"I called the dispatcher, then followed the road until I saw the sheriff's car and your horse trailer with your name on the side."

She nodded her head.

They found one of the last parking places a block away from where the parade had just started and sauntered over. People were dressed in western clothes and colorful Spanish attire. The pioneer spirit of the Old West was in full swing.

A Scottish clan marching band played an ancient Celtic song on their bagpipes and turned heads as they passed along the parade route. Matching horses high-stepped after them, their riders astride glittering silver saddles. A Native American group dressed in traditional Indian finery, with bright feathers and beads, danced along the street.

The San Juan Capistrano Soccer League followed, while vaqueros on dancing horses strutted handsomely in their wake. Then the Charros Club passed in review, with handsome buggies and a covered wagon.

Without warning, gunslingers held a mock shoot-out in the middle of the street. After the initial shock, everyone laughed and clapped, including Erin and Jordan. Mike Fury came next in the parade line, his horse equipped with working class gear. Erin shouted to get his attention. Mike doffed his cowboy hat to his daughter and rode proudly on.

Behind him a group of Regency College's students rode their horses, coming to a halt to do a short drill Erin had taught them.

"We better get out of here," Jordan said. "I'm not wearing western clothes and those guys over there on the corner in black western suits are giving me the eye. I don't want to be slapped in their makeshift jail-house."

But he was too late. Three husky men with oversized star badges, unsmiling, came up behind him and threw on handcuffs. Erin couldn't hide her laughter.

Without so much as a word, they marched him to the iron-barred jail and unceremoniously pushed him in. Erin followed them. She stood aside with her hands thrust in the back pockets of her jeans, amused, glad she'd worn a western shirt and boots.

"Tough," she said, grinning.

Jordan took it with a grain of salt. After all, it was an annual ritual, and the money went to charity. All the same, he wished he'd remembered to wear something western and avoid the hassle.

The judge rode up on a black horse and eyed him. "Either pay up or do the time, stranger," he roared. "What'll it be now?"

Jordan paid the fine good-naturedly and they released him. People standing around laughed—knowing it was all part of the show.

After the parade, they watched Spanish dancers, then took their time going in and out of the shops and the booths that lined the streets. Jordan bought her a taco from a street vendor.

When he drove her home, she said, "I had a wonderful time. Stay for supper. I put something in the crockpot this morning."

"If you're sure you have enough," he said.

"No problem."

"I've got to run an errand first, then I'll come back. Okay?"

"Sure. I'll get things started."

Erin hurried into the house and headed straight for her bedroom. Taking one look in the mirror, she wiggled out of her clothes and jumped in the shower.

After towel-drying herself, she ran a comb through her hair, then dressed, choosing a denim skirt and a white blouse.

Taking only a moment to apply lipstick, she dashed to the kitchen.

She hadn't quite finished setting the table when Jordan arrived. He handed her a bottle of red wine. It gave her a little shock to realize just how pleased she felt to see him again.

"Thanks," she said. "Was this wine your errand?"

"Didn't want to come empty handed."

She grinned. He followed her back to the kitchen.

"Can I help?' he asked.

"If you can wash romaine lettuce." She pointed to the sink. "The tomatoes are in the refrigerator."

He glanced down at the lettuce. "No spinner?"

"What's that?"

He didn't explain, just washed the green leaves and methodically pulled them apart. Then he opened the refrigerator and took out two of the reddest tomatoes he'd ever seen. "From your garden?"

"Vine ripe. Dad grows them. He's got a green thumb."

Erin sounded a little frazzled. She handed him a bowl for the salad and grabbed a big spoon out of a drawer. He cut the tomatoes into quarters and added dressing that he found on the inside of the refrigerator door.

"You know your way around a kitchen," she said, taking a moment to observe him, her tone more relaxed.

He leaned against the counter, one hand stuffed

complacently in his trouser pocket, his gaze holding hers firmly. "We bachelors have to eat, too."

"Are you always so sure of yourself?"

"Let's be friends," he said.

She smiled. "Actually, I kind of like having you around."

His slate-gray eyes leveled warmly on her. "Good friends are hard to come by."

Erin lifted her chin. "Friends, then."

Still, she was afraid to feel too much, to care too much for this man.

"Everything's about ready," she said, changing the subject. "I'll call Dad."

Before she could turn away, he reached out, his hands closing around her arms, and pulled her into an embrace. Erin's breath altered with his touch and she widened her eyes, examining his features.

After a moment, she backed away, laughing. "Supper's ready."

Her father came in and they sat down, a smile on his lined face. She found it hard to concentrate with Jordan so close—the clean scent of his soap, the way he'd carefully combed his hair.

Mike spoke up. "Erin said you were in Sacramento a couple of days ago."

He passed the salad to Jordan.

"Yes. I think it was a worthwhile trip. By the way, you and your horse looked great in the parade today."

Mike's face lit up. "Thanks's. It's a yearly thing, and I enjoy participating. The swallows always return to the mission about this time. Kinda' nice having a celebration in their honor."

Jordan felt more at ease as he took up his fork.

Maybe it was because Erin's father didn't seem ready to pounce. The man had even smiled.

Erin's baked chicken and homemade biscuits tasted good. He sipped the wine, catching Erin's inquisitive eyes peering over the rim of her glass at him.

"I bet you made a good impression in Sacramento," she said.

The corners of her eyes crinkled, and she gave him an encouraging look, as though she wanted him to go on. But he didn't like tooting his own horn, even if he'd been the keynote speaker at the conference.

Erin speared a carrot and placed it in her mouth. Jordan admired her cooking. He was about to ask a question when the telephone on the kitchen wall rang. She pushed back her chair and hurried across the floor.

Cupping the receiver to her chest, she said, "It's Stu, Dad. Pirate Lady is about to foal. We better get over to his barn right away." Then she shifted to Jordan. "Sorry about this. But I'm afraid we've got to rush off."

This could get to be a habit, Jordan thought. "Wait for me. You may need an extra hand."

Chapter Eight

Mike Fury drove onto Stuart's ranch and parked in front of the weather-bleached barn. Erin and Jordan followed him inside. A kerosene lamp, hanging from a beam overhead, cast eerie shadows in the corners.

Pirate Lady stood in one of the stalls, ears shifted toward them, tail raised.

They exchanged hellos with an uneasy Stuart.

Mike pointed to the mare and said to Jordan, "That tail's a clear indication labor's started."

Jordan nodded. Stuart turned his attention back to the mare. He'd supplied her with fresh water and feed. Clean straw was scattered on the floor of the stall.

"I hope it doesn't take much longer," Stuart said, rubbing his big palms on his jeans.

"What can we do to help?" Erin asked.

Jordan didn't miss the look of adoration Stuart gave her.

"Just give me moral support," he said. "It's the Lady's first foal, and for that matter, mine too." He gave Erin a simple grin. "She's healthy. And the vet's on call, just in case there are any complications. You never can tell."

"We'll say a little prayer that everything goes well."

"Thanks for coming over. Really appreciate it."

"No problem," Mike said. "We're glad to help out."

Erin brought more fresh straw and scattered it around the stall. Jordan stood back. Now that he was here, he didn't have the first idea how he could lend a hand.

Pirate Lady gave a groan and glanced around at her flanks. Then there followed a bearing down, followed by the labored sounds of her breathing.

They waited, all eyes on the mare as her contractions grew stronger, leaving her fidgety. Her water broke and the miracle of the birth began with the foal's head and shoulders making its first appearance. The mare grunted and her sides heaved. Wrapped in a white membrane sack, the little animal emerged.

Pirate Lady laid down on her side, head up, and instinctively licked and nuzzled the foal clean. Then after awhile she rose, weak from the ordeal, and encouraged the foal to struggle to his feet. Though fragile, the little stallion immediately searched for her teat.

"Look how hearty he is already," Erin said.

They nodded.

The foal took his first drink of colostrum as those gathered around began to talk all at once.

"The next four hours are critical," Mike said. "Fortunately, no abnormalities or behavioral disturbances seem to be in evidence as yet."

"And his eyes are clear," Erin said.

Stuart looked relieved, his face more relaxed. "You won't need to stay," he said. "Both the foal and Pirate Lady look shipshape."

"We'll stick around a bit," Erin said. "Just in case you need us."

Mike leaned against a fence post. "Better to be on the safe side," he said, nodding.

Erin found a rake and worked to clear the soiled straw away from the mare and foal, stirring up the birth smells. Stuart hurried to bring clean straw.

"I'll go get a pizza and a thermos of coffee," Jordan offered. "It looks like it's going to be a long night." He wished he could be of some real help.

Oblivious to the people and their concerns, the mare leaned her graceful neck down and groomed the foal with her tongue. Jordan had never seen a foal born. It was awesome.

The next day Erin and Sarah Whitefeather took Josh to see the foal. The boy couldn't take his eyes off the small fellow. Stuart had hardly left the mare and the foal alone since the birthing. It showed in the circles under his eyes.

"Can I ride him when he gets older?" Josh asked.

"Maybe," Stuart said. "But I'll let you name him. Be thinking about it and let me know when you've decided."

Josh's eyes snapped wide with sheer joy. "You mean it?"

"Why not?" Stuart tousled the boy's hair. "Come

on. Let's get some of that special feed for Lady Pirate. I've never seen her so hungry."

After they had gone, Sarah said, "And Jordan stayed the whole time?" Her forearms rested on the fence railing.

"Don't ask me why," Erin replied.

"I've known you for years and I never saw you look at a man quite that way."

"Don't be ridiculous."

"Ridiculous? I don't think I'm far off. By the way he looks at you, I can tell he cares about you," she said wistfully. "Harry used to look at me that way." A tremor seeped into her voice. "That is, before he learned we had a disabled son. I guess he couldn't take it."

Erin patted her arm. "I'm sorry. That had to be doubly hard on you."

"I'm over it now," she replied too quickly. "Oh, gosh, why did I have to bring that up and get all maudlin? I couldn't be luckier to have Josh for a son."

"Absolutely," Erin agreed. "Harry's the big loser. Lost you and that great kid."

Stuart and Josh returned with a bucket of feed. A weary smile played over Stuart's lips.

"You look tired but content," Sarah told him.

"It's like being a real father," he said. "Erin was here until all hours, too. But I think she's too pretty to show any exhaustion."

Erin was taken aback by the unexpected compliment and swallowed hard. Trying to make light of it, she said, "You've got that right."

He chuckled.

Sarah glanced from one to the other, then turned her

attention to Josh. "We better be getting along, tiger. Can't have you late for school."

"Come by any time," Stuart said. Then he slanted a glance at Josh. "Don't forget to think up a real good name. I'd hate to think this little fella' never got a decent name because it slipped your mind."

Josh grinned. "I won't forget."

A few days before the board meeting was scheduled, Jordan met with John Herrington, the chairman. Herrington was a short, geeky-looking type with overly big ears and glasses sliding down his nose. Things weren't going well. Jordan thought the man was a thick-headed egomaniac in love with power, as well as being the world's worst nit-picker. They'd had some run-ins before. He knew Erin Fury could be willful and contrary too, and likely to thumb her nose at the board if she didn't hear what she wanted. For her sake, he hoped things went smoothly.

Herrington looked at Jordan, his mouth pinched. "I don't like these delays," he grouched in flat vowels.

Jordan sat across the desk from the man. He'd tried to make a case in favor of the Furys. But how could he possibly get him to understand the Furys tended to matters of the heart, in a dot-com world?

Herrington growled, "I can't understand your change of attitude, Archer. I thought you wanted to get rid of that stinky manure pile over there." He looked sharply at Jordan with wizened eyes. "I've seen Erin Fury on that horse of hers. Pretty little thing. Tell me, has the young woman come to mean something to you? Is that what this is all about?"

Herrington's remarks came out of no where, Jordan

thought with a scowl. But he controlled his rising temper. "This is not about liking or not liking the Furys. At the time I suggested the lease not be renewed, I wasn't aware of the service the ranch performs for the community. It would only be good public relations to extend the lease for, say, another five years. They are well known and popular. Some of our own students board horses at the stables and are quite involved in volunteering over there."

Herrington did not look pleased as his manicured fingers tapped the expensive desk. Jordan frowned. He knew Herrington carried a lot of sway with the other trustees. He pictured them siding with him like a kangaroo court.

Jordan tried to keep the edge out of his voice. "It's in our interest to postpone the building plans until this has been thoroughly researched. Besides, there's that property down the road we have an option on."

Herrington's eyes narrowed. "The land use hasn't been explored for that piece of land yet."

"Just hear the Furys out," Jordan said with determination.

"Well, isn't that what we're going to do? You know I'm an open-minded man."

"Thanks, John. I think you'll be impressed by them."

Herrington didn't reply.

Erin and her father arrived for the informal board meeting, accompanied by Sarah and Stuart. Jordan watched them enter the building, wishing he could go up to them and say hello. But he only nodded, wanting to appear impartial, knowing his job could hang on this. It didn't do to antagonize one's employers.

Stuart seemed to always be around, Jordan thought irritably. Though a nice enough guy, Jordan couldn't help feel a twinge of envy. He knew Erin counted on him more than she realized. They seemed to have the kind of relationship that wouldn't be too difficult to change into something more meaningful. And Jordan wasn't quite sure how far their alliance had progressed when he'd first met her.

Stuart and Sarah stayed in an outer room while Erin and her father came in. After introductions, everyone took their seats around a table and the meeting got underway. Jordan tried hard to look impassive. Out of her customary jeans and wearing a dress, Erin was the most adorable creature he'd ever seen. Seated across from her, the table distanced them more than he wanted to think. Strain marked Erin's face by the tightening of her mouth. He threw her a slight smile but she didn't respond. He felt edgy, not holding out much hope for them.

Why was he letting this happen, knowing Herrington's bent, but what could he do to change it at this point. For years Jordan had prided himself on his fairness, although he had a driving determination that could get in the way. Now, because of him, the college trustees were about to rob the Furys of their livelihood, legal though it might be. It was like being sheared of his humanity in one fell swoop. His old college buddies, scattered now, always said he was a pretty cool customer, and teased him about his eagerness to make a name for himself. Well, he'd been there, done that. And what did it get him?

After meeting Erin Fury, things had changed fast. Watching her now, he felt deeply moved by her resolve and courage in facing the stern men.

Erin sat quietly, looking outwardly calm, but underneath he knew she was a bundle of nerves, just like himself. Her deep russet hair was swept back, held in place by silver combs. She wore a becoming red dress—the power color. Did she wear it on purpose? A slender shaft of light from the window fell across her face. He noticed with sadness the paleness under her tanned cheeks. Her father swiped a hand across his forehead and frowned, his face flushed. He looked sorely out of place in an outdated polyester suit and cowboy boots.

Herrington put a stock actor's smile on his face and continued the spiel about how he understood their dilemma. Jordan checked his wristwatch and shifted in the chair. He felt like he was on a bus about to careen off a precarious cliff. The meeting dragged on. He wished he could say something, but he'd already argued with the trustees behind closed doors.

When the man finally shut up, Erin gave a persuasive argument for the Furys staying on the land. She listed all the benefits the ranch performed for the community and told them about the children who would be the losers if the Furys were forced to leave.

"We've always given lessons to these disabled children at no charge. It's a great advantage to them. Just ask their parents. We also find good homes for horses who are abandoned or whose owners can't keep them. We board some of your students' animals, too. What will happen to our worthwhile programs if we fold? We invite you to join hands and help support us."

Then Mike Fury spoke in a no nonsense tone of voice. Jordan could tell by his eyes he'd like to take a poke at Herrington. But he finished what he'd come to say and sat back rigidly in the chair, his big hands folded.

The chairman stood and spoke in a flat, nasal voice. "We have listened to your arguments, and certainly they have merits. However, you must understand the college's expansion comes first. This is a fine institution of higher learning. We *also* perform a service. Now, if you'll step outside for a few minutes, we will discuss this." His mouth went limp and he sat back down.

Erin and her father filed out, joined by Stuart and Sarah. Jordan barely kept his smoldering temper under wraps once they closed the door behind them. He loosened his tie, wanting to choke Herrington for the small-minded man he'd shown himself to be.

In the outer room, Erin's blood boiled at the man's petty oratory. She glanced at her father. His world was about to crash on top of him and from his look he knew it all too well.

"If they'd just give us another year," she said, "instead of acting so cavalier."

"Herrington's crewcut is stiffer than prom hair," Sarah said with a mischievous wink. "I'd like to take my lawnmower to it."

Erin gave a nervous chuckle.

Then they were called in. The members leaned back in their seats, sipping coffee and talking among themselves. John Herrington cleared his throat noisily.

"We've come to a joint conclusion that delaying our plans would be an inconvenience and would not be in our interest. We must go ahead with our project. We're sorry to have to confirm this decision, which had, in any event, already been reached several weeks ago."

"You can't do this," Erin pleaded.

Herrington sniffed through the legal papers like an old hunting dog who's unearthed a rotten bone, and his brows thickened. "Miss Fury, please! We've made this all quite clear to you and your father. There's no further need to continue. This meeting is adjourned."

The board members rose to leave, not making eye contact with the Furys.

Mike sputtered, "You're a bunch of overgrown toads—the bunch of you." Then he gave them a cold shoulder.

From the devastated look on Erin's face, Jordan could see the chasm between them growing wider than the Grand Canyon. The realization broke as clearly and bleakly as the ball-point pen mark on Herrington's expensive, tailored white shirt.

Erin swore under her breath and glared across the table at Jordan. He had deliberately set out to fool them from the very beginning, she told herself angrily. That explained his sudden interest in the first place. It was only calculated trickery. For some insane reason he'd wanted to make the peasants think he was some sort of Robin Hood. Ha! What did he think they might do, when he held all the cards?

Her father had always taught her to face down fear, but she was too shocked to feel anything more than gut-wrenching wrath. Jordan's stricken face had no effect on her.

Tight-lipped, Erin raised her nose and stared at Jordan. "You knew all along the committee wouldn't relent," she said through clenched teeth. "This has been a sham from the get-go."

Jordan blinked. "I thought they'd give you a chance if they had the opportunity to hear you out. And I did have a long talk with Herrington yesterday. I'm really sorry about this."

Jordan felt her disappointment acutely, but there was nothing more he could do. He reached over to take her hand but she pulled away as though he were some kind of viper and marched to the door, Mike Fury one boot-step behind her.

Gripping the handle and swinging the door open, she pivoted back to face Jordan one last time. "You manipulated us," she said, terribly hurt, "making us think you were one of the good guys, the knight in shining armor who would ride up on your charger and save us." She shook her head. "You certainly aren't the man I thought you were."

Stung by the rebuke, Jordan lifted his eyebrows. "Erin, you're wrong. Please listen."

Her eyes flashed, and he saw the agony mixed with hostility.

"I'm not blind, Mr. Archer," she snapped coldly.

"But . . ." His voice trailed. What could he say, not feeling very heroic at that moment.

In a menacingly low tone, Erin said, "I don't want to see you again—ever!"

"You don't mean that," he said, wanting to reason with her.

Erin dabbed at the corners of her eyes and her voice cracked. "Yes, I do, Jordan!"

Stuart stepped forward and took her arm. "Come on, Erin."

Jordan stood quite still, not speaking. Her words hit like a jagged glacier. He looked at her and shook his head. This couldn't be happening, he thought grimly.

"Good-bye, Jordan," she said, her voice barely audible. She turned on her heel and walked away with Stuart, her shoulders back, head held high. Her father took her hand, his jowls waggling with pent-up rage. Sarah trooped along behind the three of them.

Jordan was too stunned to react. His eyes burned. Nothing he said would get through at this moment. He decided to let her cool off. Then he'd go over to the ranch and make her listen to him.

She was being foolish. Didn't she know how hard he'd tried? Give him some credit!

"We owe a debt to these people who hang on to the county's historic roots," he'd told Herrington fervently. "The Fury Ranch is one of the few remaining. Do we really want to pave over this entire valley with concrete buildings and asphalt?"

But the man had been unimpressed. The verdict wasn't unexpected, either. Worst of all, he'd dashed the Furys' hopes.

Erin's jaw set. She and her father packed into the Cherokee. Stuart and Sarah climbed in the back, and Mike drove them silently away from the college parking lot.

By the time Erin arrived home, a sad emptiness left her feeling drained. Her image of Jordan's wounded expression lessened her defenses. Impulsively, she'd lashed out in anger, not giving him a chance to more than open his mouth. Part of her wanted to tell him she didn't mean what she said, but the other side, the proud side, needed to go on blaming him. Too much was at stake. It was, after all, his original idea. He'd never denied that.

The remainder of the day passed in a blur. She fed horses and gave horseback riding lessons. That night, exhausted, she mercifully fell into bed, hoping to escape into oblivion. But sleep fought her to a standoff as she went over and over what had happened. She wanted to give him a piece of her mind one minute and thank him for trying to help the next. Yet she couldn't bring herself to pick up the telephone and call his number. Their relationship was over. The damage bit too deeply. There could be no going back. She told herself she wouldn't miss him, and put a pillow over her head and sobbed.

In the Furys' rustic office the next morning, Erin stood looking out the open window, unable to begin her chores. An owl hooted nearby but she paid no attention. Jordan had phoned several times, coming up against a blank wall when she refused to talk to him. An intermittent rain had soaked the hills and the children couldn't ride. It would be a long day.

Her father always said her impulsiveness was her greatest flaw, that and finishing people's sentences. Of course, she inherited both traits from him, she told herself.

Erin sighed heavily. Was it impulsive to race over to the college that day when she learned the trustees weren't renewing their lease? Was it impulsive to tell Jordan she'd sell him Indian Man, thereby assuring he'd hang around? Most of all, wasn't it the height of impulsiveness to fall in love with the man. Funny, she'd never admitted that to herself.

What was the use of even thinking about love. Truth be told, she felt miserable about having spoken so harshly to him. Oh, how easily her quick tongue and independent streak could get her into trouble. Well, it was done. Yet the image of his face, his eyes narrowing, kept drifting before her own eyes to taunt her.

Sighing, she knew things could only get worse. With a stifled cry, she let her chin drop and turned away from the window.

Later on, the Santa Ana winds whipped into a frenzy, the tempo leaving Erin antsy. Sarah stopped by on her way home from work. They sat in the glider swing, tucked up away from the full force of the wind.

"My life has gotten crazy," Erin said.

"Still thinking about holding a rally?" Sarah asked.

"It's the only way. Maybe public outrage will make the board rethink their foolish decision."

"Certainly your meeting with them didn't have any effect, if you'll pardon my saying so."

"It was a sheer waste of time."

"The best way to forget your troubles is to wear tight boots," Sarah said, trying to lighten Erin's black mood.

"Not funny," Erin replied.

Stuart came out of the barn and headed toward his pickup. He'd been repairing a rafter.

"How's the foal?" Sarah called out to him.

He strolled over to them. "He's doing just fine and so is Pirate Lady. Did Josh come up with a name yet?"

Sarah chuckled. "He's down to three. Toy Box, Soldier, and Fire Fighter. But the list may have changed by the time I get home." She turned to Erin. "Got to run. My mom's baby-sitting and she's going to her book group tonight."

Stuart said, "So long," to them and headed back toward his pickup. Erin walked Sarah to her van and stood watching until both vehicles turned onto the highway. Then she kicked a pebble and tried to be more upbeat.

The next day, Stuart returned after he got off work. A computer programmer, he admitted to Erin once that he hated his work. Maybe that was why he spent an inordinate amount of time volunteering on the Fury Ranch, Erin thought. She gave him a generous smile as he followed her into the barn.

"You did a good job on those beams," she said. "Would you mind stacking the bales of hay Dad brought in this morning? He didn't do too good a job. I guess he's got a lot on his mind."

"Sure, Erin."

Stuart took her hand and folded it companionably into his own. His blue eyes shined with a sympathetic kindness that touched her heart. For a long time he'd been like a brother, always there when she needed him. Sometimes she felt guilty, taking his time away from his own family's ranch.

He placed an arm gently around her shoulders. "You and Mike have had a tough time of it lately," he murmured, his breath inches from her ear. "I only wish I could do something."

"We haven't given up yet," she stammered, his compassion nearly bringing on tears.

He lifted her chin and brushed her lips with his. The tender gesture took her by surprise but she didn't take offense. His lips were warm and loving. However, she stepped out of the circle of his arm.

"Gosh, everything's in such a mess, Stu. And the chuckwagon cookout and barn dance are coming up soon. I should be finishing up with the plans. But right now my brain's tapped out. Can't think of anything, and that's not like me."

"I'll always be here for you, Erin," he said softly.

She patted his cheek affectionately. "That's for being such a sturdy shoulder to cry on."

Then, as he released her hand, she realized Stuart always had been there like her right arm.

Chapter Nine

Sarah talked Erin into stopping for a bite at the Swallows Inn after they came out of a movie. They sat at a small table toward the back of the crowded room. Tired, Erin held her head up by planting an elbow on the tabletop. The worry over the ranch had dissipated her usual high spirits.

"That movie was too slow-paced," she said. "I thought it would be more fun."

"Yeah. Sort of boring after the middle."

With a sigh, Erin confided, "I've been so unhappy lately, Sarah."

"I know. But we're getting a lot of responses for the rally. Parents of Girl Scouts. Boy Scouts. The Sierra Club. Your own volunteers."

"Thanks for sending out all those flyers. Sometimes

138

I think it's nonsense to even gather all these people for the rally—take up their time. I certainly haven't been able to buck those hard-headed trustees."

"C'mon, Erin. Don't give up yet. You're a fighter."

Erin nodded. "I've got to keep focused on the big picture, I guess, and not let myself get distracted."

Sarah patted her hand. "I know it's darn tough."

Erin pulled herself together and cleared her throat. "You've been wonderful, Sarah." Changing the subject, she said, "Tell me, what name did Josh pick for Lady Pirate's foal?"

"Champ."

She perked up. "Champ. I like it. It has a positive ring. Are you planning to bring your guitar to the cookout?"

"Uh-huh. Josh is learning the words to some of those old cowboy songs. Now he wants to be a cowboy and live on a cattle ranch in Montana."

Erin smiled. "He'll probably get interested in rockets next."

"A rocket scientist. That wouldn't be bad," Sarah said, musing.

"We've been cleaning out the barn for the barn dance. Maybe you can come by the day before and help tie some big bows and streamers around. You're so good at it."

Sarah took a sip of her coke. "Sure."

A combo of musicians played *Elvira*, while a small group of line dancers executed the boot scoop, followed by the vine step. Erin tasted the root beer, then took a mouthful. It made her cough. She hadn't been away from the ranch in days.

The Swallows Inn was a well-known local watering

hole. Erin remembered that it had once been the setting for a Clint Eastwood movie. San Juan Capistrano, known to its citizens as San Juan, had its historic crown jewel of a mission, famous swallows, the old tavern, and a resident ghost who inhabited the dry riverbed. Erin loved the town.

She glanced around. There, across the room, stood Jordan talking to another man. What was he doing in a place like this—the highfalutin president of a lofty college? The mere sight of him gave her a jittery tummy. Even though she sensed the turmoil and conflict in Jordan, because she harbored so much of the same thing inside her, she dared not reach out to him. Better that they kept their distance from one another.

"Let's get out of here," she said, feeling awkward. "The air is cloyingly thick and it's much too crowded."

Sarah looked puzzled until she, too, spotted Jordan. "Sure." She took a last sip.

"He's probably in here trolling for women," Erin said spitefully.

Sarah laughed. They rose to leave, winding around tables on the way to the entrance. Erin held her head high, looking straight ahead.

Jordan caught a glimpse of Erin heading for the door. He wanted to knife through the patrons to reach her before she disappeared, but held back. He'd left several messages for her and she hadn't returned even one. Seeing her twisted his guts. She didn't want to see him—ever—she had said. The heated words rang in his ears.

His jaw tightened. The sight of her pretty face made him miss her all the more. Darn it, he wanted the woman to love him back, to share his life, to hold in his arms. But she had turned her back on him. Maybe it was for the best. He tried to hide what tortured him most—the fact that he'd failed her. The Fury Ranch was doomed.

His friend, Hank, an old college buddy, went on talking about a new minivan he was considering for his wife. Jordan half listened, nodding at appropriate times. The music howled like a gust of wind through his heart. He needed to get out of there fast.

Infuriating woman! Just a quick glance at her and he was all worked up. It was over between them before it barely got started. Fine! But down deep he knew he was only lying to himself. He wanted Erin more than he had ever wanted anything.

Dejected, Jordan finally said so long to his friend and drove home. He took a cold shower and stared at a loose tile on the wall. Enclosed in the shower stall, he scrubbed an elbow with a jerking motion, then stepped out and slung a towel around him.

He'd go over to Erin's the first thing in the morning, whether she liked it or not. The decision didn't help him sleep. What would he say to her? He always said he'd never become involved with a woman with a temper, and here he was, perfectly crazy about a spit-fire. She'd changed him all right—what he thought about things and what had now become important to him.

He'd made mistakes along the way, but losing Erin was the absolute worst. Well, he'd licked his wounds long enough. Patience wasn't one of his virtues. He couldn't concentrate on his work, couldn't sleep.

The following morning, Jordan dressed in chinos, a

gray shirt, and boots, then headed to the Fury Ranch, putting everything else on hold.

Stuart was filling mangers in the stables when he came in. "Where's Erin?" he asked.

Stuart's eyes darkened. "She's in the office."

Ignoring the unfriendly look, Jordan nodded and strode past the tack room to the office. He opened the door quietly and entered, closing it behind him. Seeing her, he felt more alive. She bent over and took something out of the small fridge. He stood there a moment and shifted his weight, not speaking. She looked great.

Erin glanced up and her eyes widened in astonishment. "Jordan!"

Without saying a word, he grabbed her and smothered her lips with his. She twisted her head free.

"Let go!" she demanded, pushing him away. "What's gotten into you?"

He went on the defensive. "I find the way you've been treating me just a tad above pure self-centeredness," he told her as her stubborn chin went up. "And I don't intend to let you forget I exist. You surely know I wanted in the worst way for the trustees to vote in your favor. They knew it and chose to go against my recommendation."

She straightened. "You walked away with my trust, Jordan. Then you come here and tell me how much you tried. Why should I believe you now?"

Anger seized him. Why wouldn't she listen? "You don't know the first thing about me or what I'm thinking."

Her eyes glittered. "Oh? I happen to know you're self-absorbed and overly ambitious. Apparently you let nothing stand in your way."

He pushed down the anger. "Erin, darling, listen to me. Give me a chance to explain."

"Ha!"

"Misunderstandings are corrosive. They eat up what could have been. Maybe I'm a trifle pompous. I don't necessarily like what I was becoming. But you've made me see things differently."

His words had the effect of cooling her hostility a little. "I was terribly hurt but I'll live, I guess."

"Then we can pick up where we left off?" He couldn't believe his good fortune.

"No," she said flatly. "I don't think I can go that far."

"What do you mean? I don't understand."

"My father and I have only a few weeks left here. It will take all my time and energy trying to find a new place, if it's even possible. I talked with a realtor but he just shook his head. I don't know how we'll carry on our activities." She neglected to mention the rally. He didn't need to know what they were planning.

Jordan stood, his hands to his sides. "At least let me see you," he said. "And there's Indian Man. I'm planning to come over early every morning and take care of him myself. He's mine now and I'll do the grooming. No need to take up your time. You'll let me do that?"

"It's up to you."

"You're quite a woman, Erin Fury," he said with a grin.

She gave him a half-hearted smile. "If you want to lend a hand, you can pick up a pitchfork and muck out your horse's stall now."

He glanced at his boots, glad he had worn them. "Sure. Why not?"

She chuckled. "That polish job won't last long, and you'd better tuck your pantlegs in the tops of your boots."

Jordan stepped back out into the stables. Erin followed. He was determined to win back her respect. When he caught Stuart gazing at her wistfully, it caused his jealously to work double time. She and the man had too much in common. And he knew she sometimes went places with Stuart. Okay, maybe it was only to the feedstore, but they'd come back to the ranch, their heads together in animated conversation.

The next day, Erin worked on last minute preparations for the ranch's annual chuckwagon cookout and barn dance. Mike and Stuart hauled the covered wagon out of the barn. Some of the college students came over to assist in tying colorful paper streamers to the hoops. They talked and giggled. Stuart hefted bales of hay onto the wagon's flat bed while Erin oiled the wooden wheel spokes. The barn had been cleaned and decorated for the dance, with Sarah's artistic hand, and farm tools stashed away.

"This sunkissed weather couldn't be better for the outing," Erin told Stuart and her father.

"I'm glad we decided to go on with the event as planned," Mike said. "Think of how disappointed the kids would be if we canceled it just because of our problems."

"Maybe the cookout will lift all our spirits," she replied.

"Jim's been might nice, donating his ranch for our cookout and the chuckwagon year after year."

"You and Jim go way back."

"Yeah. A few years."

"Maybe like forty or so?"

He chuckled. "Since he gave me a nose bleed in kindergarten."

Erin's father came out the kitchen door. "That pot of chili simmering on the stove is the best ever. Hope I made enough for everyone."

"You always make tons, Dad. Don't worry about it." She just hoped he wouldn't make it too spicy hot.

He surveyed the wagon. "Looks like you've about got it ready. Let me know when you want me to hitch up the team. I see Jim rolling in with the chuckwagon. He called to say he'd checked out the ranch yesterday. Everything seems in good order since he and his wife moved into town."

Erin nodded. "Stu and I will ride on ahead just as soon as all the families get here and the children and their folks are settled in the wagon."

Stuart stood up and stretched his back. He'd been checking the wagon and doing last minute chores. A quiet, forthright man, Erin valued his friendship.

"We're about ready," he said, his eyes exploring her face.

"I hope the kids all have a grand time," she said. "Thanks for all your help, Stu. I don't know what we'd do without you."

"This has become my home away from home," he said, grinning.

Things moved along. Mike and Stuart checked the

harness and buckled leather straps while they hooked up the team. Cars and trucks arrived caravan-style, spilling out excited children dressed like cowboys and cowgirls.

Stuart received a call from home. In all the chaos, he turned to Erin. "My kid brother called. The foal's sick. I'll need to go take a look at him. Sorry. I'm not sure I'll get back in time to ride out to Jim O'Toole's ranch with you. Darned shame, at the last minute and all."

"You go take care of Champ. God forbid if anything happened to the foal—the way Josh dotes on him. I'll be just fine."

The unhappy slant of his tanned face telegraphed his disappointment, but what else could he do? Erin finished stuffing things in her saddlebags. He hurried to his horse, jumped in the saddle and took off at a gallop through the orange grove.

Jordan arrived while the children were being loaded onto the wagon and lent a hand, then saddled Indian Man. Erin had only half-heartedly invited him but he didn't plan to miss it. The horse was more frisky than usual, sensing the commotion. College students and several other riders gathered, ready to accompany the wagon.

Jordan rode up to where Erin was getting ready to mount. "Mind if I ride along with you?" he asked.

She shook her head, nixing his plan out of hand. "I need you to follow the wagon, just in case of any emergencies. And make sure the kids keep seated. We don't want anyone falling out."

Frustrated, he reluctantly agreed. Mike climbed up and took a seat on the wagon, the reins resting comfortably in his big hands. The children whooped and giggled, as parents checked to make sure the things they would need were stowed on the wagon.

Erin, riding Angel Face, started down the long drive alone, thinking maybe Stuart would still catch up to her if the foal was okay.

She rode along the side of the highway at a moderate clip, thinking about her conversation with Jordan. Then she turned off onto the trail. She had tried to keep everything on a level keel since he'd been coming to the ranch early each morning to care for Indian Man. But she gave him little ground, refusing to be caught alone with him.

Erin glanced down at her watch. Thinking she could make better time by taking a shortcut down a creek bed, she turned off the trail.

Back at the Fury ranch, Mike gave the horses the signal and the wagon rolled forward, accompanied by Jim O'Toole in the chuckwagon. It looked like a scene reminiscent of the Old West. Grandparents, having come to see the children off, snapped photos and waved good-byes from the sidelines. The boys and girls hunkered down in the wagon, whispering and giggling, their parents chatting amiably with one another. Sarah Whitefeather strummed her guitar and everyone began to sing western songs. Jordan pulled his hat down lower and followed along, keeping an eye on the children, expecting some roughhousing. He joined in the singing, raising his voice to, "I'm an old cowhand, from the Rio Grande . . ."

An hour later, the wagons pulled onto the O'Toole ranch picnic grounds. The place was deserted. No

Erin. No Stuart. Mike stood up and looked around, a frown increasing the worry lines on his forehead.

He cupped his hands to his mouth and shouted, "Erin! Oh, Erin! Stu!"

No answer echoed back. Only the hushed tones of the sycamore trees shading the house murmured in the breeze, along with the call of a quail. There wasn't even a hint of anyone having been to the camp. No fresh hoof prints. No paper tablecloths arranged on the wooden picnic tables. The house, which hadn't been occupied, was locked. Jim set the brake, jumped down off the chuckwagon seat, and hurried over to unlock the door.

With a frown furrowing his face, Mike climbed down from the wagon, muttering, and helped the children clamor out the back of the wagon.

Jordan picked up an ice chest. "Why isn't Erin here?"

"Yeah," Sarah chimed in. "I thought she and Stu were supposed to be ahead of us."

Jordan could see the uneasiness growing on Mike's grizzled face. "Beats me. I hope she didn't get thrown. Stu's with her, though. He'll take care of things."

Something wasn't right. Jordan felt his skin crawl. Why hadn't he brought along his cell phone? "Maybe I should go look for them."

Mike rubbed the stubble on his jaw and stood there a moment, thinking. "I got a cell phone under the wagon seat. Carry it for emergencies. Never know when one of these kids might get sick or something. Jim doesn't have a phone out here anymore. Would you get it for me?"

Jordan sat the ice chest on a table and raced back to the wagon to retrieve the cell phone.

Here," he said, handing it over.

"I'll call home, just in case they had to turn back," Mike said, punching in the numbers.

No answer.

Then he put in a call to Stuart's home. Someone picked up the receiver. Jordan got the gist of the conversation. The foal was sick. Erin had sent Stuart back and gone on alone. Jordan's heart seemed to stop dead, then started at a fast pace. Good heavens! Erin was out by herself somewhere. From the looks of things, she could be hurt.

Jordan ran to Indian Man and leaped into the saddle. "I'll go find her," he called to Mike. "If she took the trail, we'd have come across her. Got any suggestions where I should look first?"

"Maybe she took the shortcut down the creek bed. Or she might have cut through the Landis property which borders this place."

"I'm on my way," Jordan said.

"Thanks." Mike grunted. "I've got my hands full here. Take the cell phone and call me the minute you find her."

Jordan slipped it into his saddlebag, his mind conjuring up all sorts of frightening things like mountain lions and rattlers. In an agony of nerves, he tipped his hat and tapped Indian Man's reins. The racehorse sprinted like he'd been trained to do at the track. Hooves pounded. Dirt flew. Jordan held on, experiencing the ride of his life as the horse flew across the picnic grounds.

Chapter Ten

Indian Man didn't slow until a full mile had been eaten up, then the horse stopped and blew hard before settling into a ragged trot. Jordan slowed him to a walk, letting the horse cool down from the exuberant, free-spirited run. The creek bed was close by. He rode a couple of miles down its winding path and followed along the banks.

Squinting his eyes, he surveyed the territory ahead. Troublesome thoughts plagued him. Anything could happen out here—a rattlesnake, her horse tripping in a gopher hole. She had to be somewhere near. He called her name several times but received no reply.

Jordan sighed heavily, thinking about her. *You plan. You build. Then a woman like Erin Fury comes along and you willingly throw away everything you've put together just to be with her*. Those thoughts made him smile.

Did she have any idea just how much he wanted her? He stood up in the stirrups, cupped his hands to the sides of his mouth and shouted again, "Erin!"

Still no response.

Disappointed, he hurried the horse around the next curve. It brought him deeper into the creek bed as he followed a spindly stream. Then he spied her horse and his heart pounded. Erin squatted on the ground. She wore a bright red shirt that stuck out in the beige surroundings like a stop sign. Alarm sucked the breath from his chest. Was she hurt? She looked up and relief flooded over him.

"You found me," she said. "How did I know it would be you doing the searching?"

He jumped down. His forehead puckered. "Are you hurt?"

A dove warbled an answer before Erin could reply. "I'm okay, but Angel Face threw a shoe. I can't ride her over this rocky terrain. Might split a hoof. Believe me, it's been a long walk. I thought we'd stop for a rest." She cocked her head, took off her hat, and mopped her brow with the back of her hand, turning her gaze from him to the mare.

He couldn't believe how relieved he felt. She looked absolutely beautiful sitting there. His cowgirl. He wanted to sweep her up in his arms, but held back on the impulse. She could be terribly independent, and they were just now getting back on real speaking terms.

Erin had pulled off her boots, giving her feet a cool furlough. She wrapped her hand around her toes and massaged them. "These boots were definitely not made for walking."

He grinned, thinking of the old Nancy Sinatra song.

Overhead, with flashing wings spread out, a handsome raven sprang from a gnarled oak tree beside the creek bed and soared toward the sundrenched mountains. Jordan watched it go, then turned back to Erin. He still yearned to take her in his arms and reassure himself she was not harmed. Instead, he rubbed her cheekbone with his fingers.

"You're self-reliant, all right, Erin," he said, "but didn't you know we were all worried about you?"

"No need. Dad raised me to take care of myself. I wasn't lost or anything."

He looked her over with an admiring eye. "I don't doubt that for a minute."

She chuckled. The breeze caught a wisp of her hair and teased it against her nose. He pushed it away, observing the details of her face.

"The thought occurs to me that maybe we could just stay here in the creek bed and have a good talk— forget all about the cookout. But I don't suppose that would be right," he said.

"Dad needs our help, since Stu's probably not coming."

Erin arched a foot and pulled on one boot, then the other. Then he helped her up, but he didn't release her right away. His fingers caressed the nape of her neck, his lips gently covered hers, and he welcomed the soft pressure of her response.

Coming up for breath, Erin murmured, "Jordan . . ." without going on.

He gently traced the outline of her lower lip with

his thumb. "I love you, darling," he whispered with a tender passion.

Erin took a moment. "Jordan, you know how I feel. I care deeply for you but . . ."

His eyes locked with hers. "There you go again. Don't push me out of your life. Love this heartfelt isn't meant to be chained to things neither of us can change."

He kissed her again, tasting the delicious response of her body melding into his as though she were heaven sent. Her warm breath caressed his ear, making him tingle with desire.

Then she stepped away, and her voice broke when she spoke. "I wish everything was different and I didn't have to deal with all these mixed emotions. You'll have to give me a little space, Jordan. This isn't a good time for us. Don't you see?"

"No, I don't see. You're so determined. Well, it won't work to keep me at arms length. I'll keep on bugging you until you understand what I'm trying to tell you."

She shook her head but managed a smile, sending him double messages.

"We better go on now. As you said, Dad will be worried about me."

Then he remembered the cell phone. "You can call him right now."

Trying not to think of his disappointment, he took out the cell phone from the saddlebag and handed it to her.

She glanced down at the phone, then up to him. "I just thought of something. This won't do us any good.

If Dad gave you this one, it means he doesn't have one for us to call in on. We'll just have to hurry."

He threw his head back and laughed at his own stupidity. "What a blockhead I am. Why didn't I think of that?" But he had been too concerned about Erin to think rationally.

She laughed too, an infectious sound that intoxicated him. The curve of her smile made him want to kiss her again but there was no time.

"You'll have to be my caboose," he said.

"I've ridden double before."

Reluctantly, he swung into the saddle and helped her up behind him.

A jackrabbit scurried across the path as Jordan turned Indian Man to where her horse was tied to a bush.

Erin let go of Jordan with one hand and took up Angel Face's reins. The mare followed obediently.

"Rumor has it that you have a secret admirer," he said, smirking.

Erin adjusted her sitting position on the horse's rump. "Oh? Who?"

"Me."

She laughed shyly. His words sounded corny but he was glad to hear her laugh. Indian Man moved on with a flick of his tail. Erin held on to Jordan to steady herself, increasing the pressure most pleasurably on his middle. Later on he'd tell her about how this rescue began with the racehorse sprinting out of the camp, nearly causing Jordan to tumble. But for now it felt good to have her so close. He'd just enjoy the moment.

They followed the trail out of the creek and along a canyon. Beyond an outcropping of rock, they came to the edge of the Landis property and followed the barbed-wire fence until it ended. Then they switched over to the edge of the O'Toole Ranch.

When Jordan and Erin reached the camp grounds, she slid off the thoroughbred's back and tied up the mare.

"Thanks for the ride," she said, smiling up at him.

He touched the brim of his hat, cowboy style. "No problem, ma'am," he drawled like John Wayne. She laughed.

The children were feeding a fat, gray squirrel. The little animal took one look at Jordan and darted up a tree. Seeing Erin, the children clustered around her, asking questions. Did she fall off her horse? Did she see any outlaws lurking about? Did she think she'd never see them again?

Mike rose to his feet and gave Erin a bear hug. He'd been cranking the handle of an old-fashioned ice cream maker, the kind that made the very best ice cream in the world. Perspiration dripped from his brow.

Erin thanked Jordan for coming after her, then buried herself in supervising a game of tag with the children. Along with the parents, Jordan assisted wherever he was needed. He watched the ebb and flow of the afternoon, not able to keep his eyes off Erin for any extended period of time. Her peppy way of walking delighted him. Everyone, including Josh, gathered around the chuckwagon to help with the cookout. The boy told his friends and fellow riders about naming Pirate Lady's foal, feeling pretty proud of himself. Jordan smiled.

Erin spent her time helping the children add leaves

and wildflowers to their collections. Prizes would be given for the best. Josh found an unusually sharp stone and everyone said it was surely an arrowhead. He showed it to Erin. After examining it, she agreed, then handed it back to the excited boy. He gave her a lopsided grin, slipping the stone in his pocket.

Jordan understood that children needed to feel special, and he wondered where Josh's father was. Erin wiped away a smudge of mustard on Josh's chin when he finished a hot-dog. Then she lined up the children for another game. Jordan entered into the fun, having a good time. He couldn't remember when he'd last felt so carefree.

Sarah took a batch of kites out of the wagon for the kite contest. Parents had helped the children make them. Colorful kites soon dipped and twisted in the clear blue sky. A lady bug landed in Erin's hair and she reached up, feeling around for it. Jordan lifted the little creature out and let it wander across his palm. When it flew away, Erin gave him a grateful smile that sent a warm glow through him.

A devilish thought occurred to him, and he whispered it to her. "What if I kidnap you and we ride off to a peaceful, secluded glen?" He grinned, knowing it wasn't going to happen. Not here. Not today.

"Another time," Erin said with a smile.

She went on working with the children, helping them sort out small arguments and petty peeves as the afternoon wore on and they grew tired. Finally it was time to return to the ranch for the barn dance. They loaded up. Soon the hills and valleys would be awash with the pastel colors of a rainbow.

Jordan recalled those, long, languid Sundays of his

youth spent cheerfully idling away his time. He knew the children gathered in the wagon had spent a happy day and would commit their own experiences to memory as he had done.

Erin watched Jordan talk and joke easily with the children and their parents as they finished loading the wagon. He seemed to fit right in. He had helped her father with the barbecue earlier and listened to Josh's retelling of finding the arrowhead. Erin grinned. Jordan was such a chameleon, knowing a lot more about things than he ever let on.

Jordan rode up on Indian Man. She was tying the mare's reins to the back of the wagon. "Want to ride along back with me?" he asked Erin hopefully.

"Thanks, but I think I'd better go in the wagon with the others," she said, although his offer tempted her.

"Let the wagons roll," Mike called, standing up and flicking a whip above the horses' backs.

Sarah played the guitar and sang an Indian song with a strong, plaintive voice. Then everyone joined in the next song, including Jordan, his deep bass voice carrying melodically through the encroaching twilight.

The two wagons lumbered along, creaking and groaning, as the teams retraced their way back to the Fury Ranch. The outside lights were on when they arrived. Stuart stood on the porch. Erin waved. Something curious glowed in his eyes. He was a stalwart, loyal man who kept a low profile and his thoughts to himself.

"You all have a great time?" he asked in his soft-spoken voice as everyone began to pile wearily out of the wagon.

They responded with smiles and comments. The

children all talked to Stuart at once. Then some of the families headed home while others waited for the barn dance to get underway. Stuart helped Mike unharness the team and led the tired horses away to the stables to be fed and watered.

The musicians were already playing when Erin entered the people-crammed barn. People were dancing and chatting in little groups. Sarah danced the two-step with Josh. She waved happily to Erin. Mike was dancing with a short, plump widow who went to their church. The two were deep in conversation.

Erin wore a forest green, velour dress that swirled around her ankles. She let her hair hang loose and pulled it away from her face with silver barrettes. She wanted to look feminine tonight, instead of her usual tomboy self, and was even wearing a light blush and lipstick.

Stuart joined her. "You look lovely, Erin," he said. "Can I get you a glass of punch or a sandwich?"

"Not yet," she replied. "How's Champ?"

"He's fine now. Sorry I couldn't be with you today. I feel really bad about it."

"No problem." She shared her experiences of the day and laughed. "You wouldn't think Angel Face would throw a shoe since the farrier checked her only last week."

He didn't look amused. "I should have been there."

"C'mon, Stu. It wasn't your fault. Things like that happen. Besides, Jordan came to the rescue."

He didn't hide the grimace very well. "Just the same, I shouldn't have let you go alone."

She knew there was no point in arguing and let the matter drop.

"Want to dance? he asked.

"Sure, if I can remember how." She chuckled. "I'm good at stepping on shins, if you remember from last year."

"It never happened."

Stuart took her hand and drew her close as the country-western musicians belted out a song. His palm held her back firmly as his free hand wrapped around hers. He was deft on his feet. They danced among the crowd and she turned her head to say hello to several friends. His admiring gaze focused on her lips.

"Having a good time?" he asked.

His breath teased her ear. "Yes," she said.

All of a sudden Erin felt the new intimacy between them and wasn't sure how to handle the situation.

"I adore you, Erin," he said, his eyes yearning. "You mean a lot to me."

She was at a loss as to what to reply. "It's nice of you to say that, Stu. I like you too."

"Keeping my eyes off you isn't easy," he said with a depth of feeling that stunned her. "Do you think we might hang out together sometime? You know—like go to a show?"

She felt her body tense. His lips were inches from hers. "Uh, Stu, I think you're a great guy, and I've always thought of you as a good friend, but I don't think of you in that way. Sorry."

His mouth turned down and he looked hurt.

"Oh, geez, I'm sorry I didn't say it better," she said. "You've been a big help to us. I don't know what we'd do without you, but . . ."

"You're not in love with me, is that it?"

"I guess you said it better than I could."

"Someone else, then?"

"I'm afraid so."

"Jordan Archer?" he asked in a strained voice.

"I wish I could say no, but how could I not be honest with you? Yes—Jordan Archer."

"If he doesn't make you happy, he'll have me to contend with."

"Thanks, Stu. Can we still be friends?"

He shrugged. "Why not?" The music stopped. He took her back to the sidelines. "Want that punch now?"

"That would be nice."

He left her standing there among the crowd. Jordan walked up.

"Here you are." He grinned. Then in a low voice, he said, "I saw you dancing with Stu. Made me jealous as all get-out."

She smiled. "Hi."

"Want to dance?"

"Not just yet."

Stuart came back with the punch. He nodded to Jordan, then sauntered away, almost before Erin had a chance to thank him. She felt awful. Stuart was such a fine man. Rejecting him wasn't something she took lightly.

She drank the punch, talking about the day's happenings.

"Let's dance," Jordan said.

Erin nodded and set the half empty glass on a table. He took her in his arms. Why were his arms so much more welcoming than Stu's? Stuart was like her, one of their own. Why couldn't she have fallen in love with him, instead of Jordan? It would make so much more sense.

Jordan held her tighter. Being with him made her heart skip wildly. No other man could do that to her.

Jordan twirled Erin around, then brought her back to him, holding her so close she could barely breathe.

"You're a remarkable woman, Erin Fury," he said, "and I'm crazy about you."

"You're pretty remarkable yourself." Her voice was barely a murmur. She nuzzled her face into the crook of his neck and would have kissed him if she thought no one was looking. The pressure he exerted on her back increased, firm and persuasive.

"I missed your sweet smile," he whispered. "I want you, need you."

She grinned. "We've only been apart for an hour or so."

His strong hand wandered up her back. " "You're a blazing sun that melts my heart, and I want to kiss you right here and now. Let's step outside," he said with a feeling that startled her.

She cleared her throat. Her pulse raced and she let her gaze roam over his face. "I wouldn't trust myself."

He pulled her close again. She couldn't see his slate gray eyes, only the curly chest hair peeking over the button of his shirt.

"Erin, darling."

The moment had her ready to give in, when someone tugged on her elbow. Thinking it to be Stuart, she looked up, then down when a familiar child's voice said, "Cuts."

Josh gave her a one-sided grin. "My turn."

Jordan released her, albeit reluctantly, his eyes momentarily darkening. Then he recognized the boy. "I know when I've been bested," he said, smiling with a glint. "But I get the next one."

Erin laughed to ease the tension. "And the next dance after that if you play your cards right. But for now Josh and I are going to take a spin around the floor."

Glistening sunlight seeped through the canopy of orange trees when Erin rose from her bed the next morning and peered out the window. Spring brought out a profusion of the daintiest flowering blooms in the garden. The heavy wisteria hanging from the trellis seemed to have unleashed its grape-like flowers overnight. A bumblebee darted in and out, then landed on a pale lavender blue petal.

Erin thought about Jordan as she slipped into blue jeans and a tank top, knowing she held his heart, yet what would she do with this gift? Avoiding him had been fruitlessly unbearable. He'd lassoed her affection with his soft endearments. Her loving inclinations were to forgive him and start over. One day she was hopelessly in love with him. But something might happen to make her hate the sight of him the next. Things surely needed to be resolved between them.

Then she thought about Stuart and what he'd said at the dance. Why hadn't she seen before that he cared for her? He'd always been there, even though she'd thought their relationship bordered on brotherly and sisterly affection. Now he was hurt, and she felt bad.

Erin cooked breakfast for her father. He had gotten

up later than usual. After eating his bacon and eggs, he stood up, looking happier than usual.

"I'm going out to the barn to start tearing down the streamers," he said with a smile. "The cookout and barn dance was grand, don't you think, girl?"

"Glad to see you in such high spirits. And I agree. By the way, who was that woman you were dancing with?" she teased.

He chuckled. "Which one?"

She laughed. "Oh, go on."

He sauntered out the kitchen door, humming.

Erin had put an apple pie on to bake before breakfast and now slipped stew meat and vegetables into the crockpot before clearing away the dishes. Glancing down at the floor, she decided to mop before going to the stables. Housework wasn't her cup of tea but duty called.

Ten minutes later, Jordan tapped on the screen door and poked his head in. He caught Erin on her hands and knees in the middle of the floor, her feet wet and bare, hair hanging in her face. She pushed a bucket of soapsuds aside and looked up.

"Got a cup of coffee left in that big pot?" he asked, giving her a broad grin.

She motioned him in. "I might be able to squeeze out one if you'll help me get to my feet."

He offered her his hand. She pushed the hair out of her eyes and made an attempt to tidy it by looping the strands at the base of her neck. He took a seat at the table, glancing around. "Glad I didn't walk across the part you just scrubbed."

"I'd have made you do it over again." she said, placing the bucket of water in the sink.

"Had a good time last night," he said.

She avoided his eyes and adjusted her tank top. "I can't believe so many people came."

"You were the best part of it."

He reached out, drew her to him, and plunked her on his lap. His arms folded her into a warm cocoon. Her hands slipped around his neck as his lips covered hers.

The screen door opened, bringing them quickly out of the intimate interlude. Erin jumped off his lap, blushing.

"Just came back to get a pair of scissors," her father said. He strode across the floor. If he noticed the goings-on, he didn't let on. "Hi. Jordan. Didn't see your car outside."

Jordan was already standing by the sink. He coughed lightly. "Hello, Mike. That was some party you threw last night."

"Yeah. It was a fine bash." Mike retrieved the scissors from a drawer and turned to go. "See you around."

Her father's appearance broke the romantic spell. Erin hurried to the kitchen range and opened the oven door. The fruit pie bubbled—ready to be lifted out—filling the room with its delicate aroma. She turned off the fire.

"Hand me the potholders in that drawer," she said.

He complied. She removed the pie to a cooling rack on the countertop.

Watching her work, Jordan could hardly contain his exuberance. Being in her presence had a way of doing that to him. With all their differences, he knew Erin was a risk worth taking. He wanted to dance with her across the linoleum, go on an extended picnic, take her sailing. His crazy thoughts made him grin.

She handed him a cup of coffee. "What are you grinning about?"

"The wild things you make me want to do."

"Maybe I better not ask and just pass on that one."

He laughed. "Seriously, yesterday was great. I can't remember ever having such a good time."

"Me, too. And you handled Indian Man well when you came to get him."

"Thanks." Then he told her about the thoroughbred taking off like a whirlwind when Jordan left O'Toole's ranch.

She laughed. "I'm glad you didn't land on your head."

He glanced over at the pie. "Do you suppose I could come back for a slice of that? We bachelors crave home cooking."

"I might be persuaded."

He remembered they'd talked about sailing a while back.

"How about going sailing with me Saturday morning? You said you'd like to sometime."

She hesitated. "Saturdays are always busy for me."

"Let one of your volunteers fill in for you for a few hours," he encouraged.

"If we could go early and I can be back at the ranch by noon or so."

"Fine with me."

"I'm afraid there's just one more condition. Will you give me a hand around here before we go? The horses have to be ready for the kids."

"What time were you thinking?"

"Oh, about six would do."

He groaned inwardly. "Okay, I'll be here."

Well, he'd try to get her back, but who could tell out there on the ocean. They might be swept away in a squall, all the way to Borneo, for all he knew.

Chapter Eleven

By seven o'clock, they were two miles out on the azure Pacific in a twenty-eight-foot sloop Jordan had borrowed from a friend. Having never sailed before, Erin was thrilled as the boat pitched and surged forward, the salt-spray in her face. Jordan reached out to tuck a stray lock behind her ear. The touch sent a shiver down her spine. Being alone with him made her feel a little shy, although she didn't know why. Maybe it was because he seemed so powerful when she wasn't in control of things.

The sloop's bow split the whitecaps one after another. Erin leaned back on the canvas cushions and crossed one knee over the other, enjoying the exhilarating experience. Jordan seemed more experienced with a sailboat than he had let on. The man was an enigma. What other hidden talents had she yet to discover?

Erin watched him work, his sinewy forearms golden in the sunlight. He took off his sunglasses and his gaze flickered over her face. Then he turned back to the lines, his long, strong fingers working hard. He set the sails while she took the rudder and did as he directed. Still, it seemed strange to see him handling the sloop with such efficiency, and herself doing nothing more than sitting there in the cockpit.

Everything secured to his liking, Jordan, dressed in khaki shorts, grasped the wheel as she tussled with a light swell. Setting the wheel due east, he slouched beside her and clasped her hand, his long legs extended, ankles crossed.

"You did just great," he said.

"Thanks for letting me play sailor."

He grinned.

The curly whorls of hair on his arms and legs were golden. She looked at the planes of his face. His generous mouth revealed him to be a sensuous man. She noticed the crowsfeet at the corners of his eyes and tiny circles at his mouth caused by sun exposure. An interesting, mobile face, she thought. Like him, she wore shorts, too, but her legs were not nearly so brown.

He tilted his head toward her. "Are you comfortable?"

"Yes. It's really very exciting being out here on the water."

"This Catalina is old, but my friend takes good care of it. He says a boat is an object made of wood, plastic or steel, that makes a hole in the water into which you pour money—spelled *break out another thousand."*

Erin laughed. She liked the shiny teakwood and brass trimmings. "What kind of boat is it?" she asked.

"An auxiliary sail boat. The sails are the main means of moving, with a small engine as a backup."

"I want to learn all about it."

"So you've never set foot on one of these before? And here you've grown up not five miles away from the shoreline."

She chuckled. "It's not like riding a horse."

He nodded. "Yeah. It's a different experience all together. If we had more time we could sail this baby all the way down to Ensenada. But there's always a next time. How about it?"

"I'd love to," she answered quietly. "At least if you fall off a boat, you land on something cushiony."

"That's debatable, and depends on a lot of things. The ocean isn't a bathtub, Erin." He looked at her steadily. She grinned back. "I love the way your nose crinkles when you smile," he said.

Just then the canvas sails billowed like white sheets on a clothesline, jerking the sloop. He reached out to steady Erin. Startled, she grabbed his arms.

"We're not capsizing," he assured her, the corners of his lips turning up. "Just luffing sails. I've got to fix them, however."

Feeling more confident, Erin closed her eyes and let the sensation of floating permeate her being as he tightened a line. She opened them to find him examining her features with rapt attention.

"You're beautiful," he said.

Erin didn't quite know how to answer his compliment except to say "Thank you." It had been a long time since anyone had called her beautiful.

He ran his hand over his shaved chin, his dark, thick eyebrows almost touching as he squinted behind his sunglasses up at the teetering mast.

Erin looked out at a large power boat, wondering if it could be called a yacht. But before she could ask, water thumped against the hull and the sloop swayed, making her stomach turn over. She didn't have her sea legs.

Jordan pointed out a whale-watching boat. A group of people, including children, stood at the rail, hopeful of spotting a school of the mammals.

"Late in the season for going out," he said. "February and March are better for whale-watching."

The raffia hat Erin was wearing proved a trial. It tried to blow away with every gust of wind. Finally, she slipped a scarf over it and tied it securely under her chin. Still, the brim whipped maddeningly against her face.

"Enough," she said. Untying the scarf, she stowed the hat behind a cushion and let the strong breeze free her hair of restraints. In no time the hat worked its way loose and danced on the tops of the whitecaps before sinking.

"Sorry," he said.

She quietly laughed. "A dolphin's probably wearing it now."

Jordan grinned. "I'll buy you a new one."

After resetting the mainsail to catch the wind, Jordan seemed in his element. He took his position beside her again, his gaze one of complete relaxation as he turned his face to the sun.

"I want to learn how to do some of those things you do," Erin said.

He took a few minutes to explain some of the basics a person needed to know about handling the sloop.

"Put your hands on the wheel like this," he said.

Erin felt the tremendous power of the water under the sloop. Jordan stood behind her and fastened his hands on the wheel with hers. His touch excited her. When she looked up at him, he kissed her temple.

With complete clarity, she knew that out here on the vast expanse of ocean they were merely two people who cared about each other. For a little while other concerns didn't matter. They were carefree, playful— having fun together in the sun.

The mainsail fluttered noisily. Erin took her hands off the wheel, and Jordan adjusted their course as she scooted out of the way.

He gave her a warm sidelong glance. "Were you always a knockout or did you wear braces and have scabby knees when you were a little girl?"

Smiling, she said, "Neither. I was awfully skinny."

"My folks thought I'd never fill out. I guess I just kept growing taller."

They sailed past Camp Pendleton, staying in their own sea lanes, and slowed to watch the Marines on maneuvers in the sagebrush-covered hills in the distance. Then they continued to cruise on down the coast until they were in sight of the few high-rises of Oceanside, a beach town.

Erin looked at her watch. "We better turn back, Jordan." She didn't realize how fast the time had flown. "It's been fun, seeing everything from this side of the world, and I've had a great time."

"I'm glad you're enjoying yourself. Want something to drink?"

"A Coke would be nice. With all this water surrounding us, you wouldn't think a person would ever get thirsty."

He took two cans out of the ice cooler, opened them, and handed one to her. She leaned back, watching his back muscles ripple under his shirt as he adjusted the sails for the return trip. When he finished, she watched him lift the can to his lips and drink.

"Do you ever feel euphoric, like everything is great with the world?"

"I've been known to," he said, giving her a half grin.

"That's how I feel right now."

He nodded agreeably. "That's terrific." Then his jaw tightened. "I'm sorry about all the misunderstandings." He paused, changing the subject. "Planning another cookout or a jamboree?"

"Nothing special."

She didn't tell him about the rally, merely talked about how Josh felt he had outgrown the pony.

He smiled. "Sounds like me at that age. I wanted to learn how to break a horse. The first time I got on one, unknown to my parents of course, the buckskin tossed me higher than a kite. I landed smack dab on my behind. Didn't try it again, either."

She laughed. "I had a similar experience. Better to let someone who knows what they're doing have the pleasure."

Jordan pointed out a tall ship making its way toward Newport Beach. The breeze grew stronger, filling the big ship's sails as it skimmed the blue water. They could see people standing on the wooden deck looking for all the world like sailors from the Eighteenth Century.

"That's the *Endeavor*," he said. "It was built to historic specifications in Australia."

"Can we follow?"

"Why not?" He raised the jib.

Erin tried to imagine what it must have been like traveling across the ocean in a tall ship. A strong gust shot them forward. Her hair whipped around her face and she raised a hand to push it away. Traveling on board the tall ship wouldn't compare with the luxury-liners of today, but nevertheless it had to have been exciting.

He noted her interest. "A fine ship," he said. "But I wouldn't have liked cruising aboard her a hundred years ago. People sometimes contracted cholera and typhus before reaching land."

She thought about what he said. Her romantic notions slipped away as a gull squawked overhead. She looked up to see two herons gracefully glide effortlessly by.

A cloud covered the sun. The air turned cold and sharp in her face and she drew her windbreaker closer around her. The tall ship outpaced them and the gap between them widened as they lost interest.

"Someday we'll sail over to Catalina Island," he said, glancing at the mound of land peeking over the horizon.

"I'd like that. It's so close, but I've never been there."

"They raise buffalo on the island. Ever have a buffalo burger?"

"No, and I'm not going to," she said crisply, breathing in the salty air.

When they reached Dana Point Harbor the sun had broken through the clouds. Erin had already helped Jordan gather in the canvases and fasten them down.

"I've had a great time," she said.

"Let's do it again soon."

"You're a man of many interests—a paradox," she said. "What else don't I know about you?"

"I think you know just about all of it."

"I doubt that very much."

Jordan slowed the engine, then maneuvered the boat into its slip. His hair fell forward on his forehead, glistening in the sun like a raven's wing. He flicked it away with a twist of his head and cut the engine. The bow gently kissed the dock and he bent down to wrap the lines around the dock cleats.

The morning had magically slipped away, and Erin was sorry to have it end.

"Am I going to barbecue you that steak dinner tonight?" he asked when they finished washing down the sails.

"I'd like that," she said smiling up at him.

He lifted her off the boat, giving her a hug.

When Erin drove to Jordan's condominium complex on a hill overlooking the ocean, the peach and lavender streaks of sunset draped across the horizon like diaphanous curtains. She set the emergency brake and walked up the path leading to his door, checking the number to be sure she had the right one. The flowered skirt she wore breezed around her ankles. She straightened the yellow tunic and reached up to touch her earlobes, satisfied she'd remembered to wear the gold loop earrings.

Erin rang the doorbell and peeked through a brass-trimmed porthole as Jordan, smiling, came to answer the door.

"Come in," he said, giving her his hand. "You look gorgeous."

She felt a lump in her throat, as if she couldn't catch her breath, and said a small "Thank you." She wished she were one of those people who always knew what to say or how to be funny and glib at the same time. He didn't take his gaze off her. Erin glanced around. She saw at once that the interior was furnished with a nautical theme. It wasn't what she had expected. The music of Andrea Bocelli played softly in the background.

Jordan noticed her interest. "I have a love of old ships—and Italian music," he said. "In that order."

"A nice combination. I had no idea." She had expected to see bookcases of scholarly tomes and furniture with the latest metal look. "I guess I don't know very much about you, after all."

He grinned.

She looked closely at a six foot tall wooden sculpture of an old pipe-smoking seafarer there in the foyer. "Your likeness?" she teased.

"Not quite. My greatest find, though."

"He's really something," she said. "I'm impressed."

He liked to hear her say that. "Take a seat on the sofa in the living room and I'll get you a drink. Iced tea?"

"That'll be fine."

Erin let her gaze wander over the interesting nautical art objects he had collected. A harpoon hung on the wall behind the sofa, along with a ship's gauge and a ship's brass plaque. The room's walls and ceiling were rough-cut cedar.

He walked back quickly, as light on his feet as an athlete, and set her wineglass on an old steamer truck used for a coffee table. Behind him, mounted on the wall over the fireplace, hung a painting of a tall-masted ship at twilight. It looked like the *Endeavor*. She commented on the artist's choice of colors and the shading.

Jordan's eyes glowed. "I'm glad you like my home."

She looked at him with awe. "Where did you find all these marvelous things?"

"In antique shops and junk stores."

He pointed out a small collection of delicately carved tiny objects in a glass-covered table beside the sofa.

"I've never seen anything like these," she said.

He opened the glass and let her examine them. He could see she couldn't resist picking up a small one the size of a pendant.

"Tell me about this," she said.

"These scrimshaw pieces are engraved or carved ivory and whalebone. In the old days, sailors did this intricate work on long voyages to pass the time. The one you're holding, the sailboat, is a particularly fine piece of work. Turn of the century, I think."

She held it up, admiring the milk-white ivory. "Simply beautiful."

"It's yours," he said.

"Oh, I couldn't keep it," she said, her eyes widening.

"It's for your birthday."

"But my birthday's already over."

She tried to hand it back to him but he covered her palm with his own. "I'll be offended if you don't keep it."

"Thank you, then. It means all the more to me because it's part of your collection."

He let go of her hand and slung his body into an easy chair across from her, picked up his glass and took a sip.

"I promised you the best darned steak in town and I've got the briquettes on right now."

"Mmm. I'm really hungry."

"Want to give me a hand in the kitchen?"

"If it will mean we can sit down to eat faster. I haven't had anything since breakfast."

"I should have brought something on the boat." He felt guilty.

"No need."

In the tiny kitchen, a bay window over the sink had shelves across the pane that held old bottles. An antique ship's lantern hung over the table, giving off a luminous light. Erin set the table.

When he brought in the succulent, aroma-teasing platter filled with steaks, she pirouetted, not holding back her exuberant pleasure. The evening was going well. She liked his condominium, his company, the gift, and now the tasty dinner they were about to eat. She was seeing him on his turf and she liked it.

After dinner, she helped him with the dishes, then

they sauntered out to the patio and continued their conversation.

"I want you to hear my new cassette," he said.

They strolled back inside. He found a Kurt Valore cassette from the movie, *I Love You, Don't Touch Me*, and slipped it on.

"Nice," she said. "Very mellow."

He took her in his arms and they slow-danced until the music ended.

"Would you like a cup of coffee, Erin?"

"Coffee's fine." She took a seat on the sofa.

Jordan returned from the kitchen carrying a tray with two mugs and set it on the trunk. This time he took a seat beside her. The nearness of her body was comforting.

"I know you want to be with me, Erin," he said simply, turning slightly to face her. "I see it in your eyes. Why don't you stay the night?"

His assertion, out of the blue, astonished her, and he wished he'd been more discrete.

"I admit to being confused where you're concerned, Jordan, but I'm not ready for that."

He framed her face in his hands, his tone intimate, his eyes locked on hers. "Let me unconfuse you, darling. You're absolutely adorable and I love you," he murmured. He let his thumb run tenderly down her throat.

A part of her couldn't believe his straightforward words. "I want to believe you, Jordan, honest I do."

His hand caressed the nape of her neck and he drew her close. His lips sought hers, searching, then demanding.

Erin felt her caution slipping away, yet managed to

pull herself together before falling into the lovely abyss. She sat up and cleared her throat. "I can't do this, Jordan. I'm sorry."

"What?"

He started to kiss her again but she turned her face away. His slate-gray eyes changed their hungry look to bewilderment. She saw the hurt there but couldn't help herself. What was the use of all this? He was on one side of the fence and she was on the other. She must be rational. If it was hard for him, it was doubly hard for her, because she loved him as well.

"Being lovers won't make things right," she muttered. "It will only complicate things."

"What things?" he asked too sharply.

"You know. I don't need to spell it out, do I?"

He dismissed the idea with a wave of his hand. "Be reasonable, darling, we love each other and . . ."

She cut him off and lifted her chin. An edge of defiance slipped into her voice. "I've taken my stand. It's my father and I against the trustees. Unfortunately, you're a part of them, Jordan."

"Erin, you know I'm trying to change that."

Panicked by her own confused doubts, she stood up and fled before he could talk her out of it.

Jordan stood there, as though planted in the floor, after Erin left. He couldn't believe she'd be so childish, so pigheaded, so uncaring. He'd tried hard to have everything just right. Darn it! He wanted her, desired her, loved her. Couldn't she see that?

An hour later, Erin sat on the side of the bed, her head in her hands, thinking about the way she'd acted at Jordan's. She made up her mind to drive back over there. What was the use of trying to keep him at arms-length? She cared too deeply for the guy, ached to hear his voice and yearned for his embrace.

The balmy spring night made her think of the passion-filled kiss he had surprised her with that first evening in the garden. It thrilled her to think of it even now.

She found a parking space and hurried to his condo. The lights were on but no one answered the doorbell's insistent ring. She thought she heard a voice coming from the patio behind the house. Maybe he was having a quiet drink out there and talking to someone on his cell phone. She hurried around the building and pushed open the gate, a smile on her face, expecting to see him reclining in a lawn chair. She tried to re-member the words she'd practiced on the drive over. It was dark, except for the lamplight slanting through the sliding glass door.

Erin walked carefully across the Bermuda grass, let-ting her eyes adjust to the faint light. Then she stopped dead. A woman was talking urgently to Jordan. Her arms slid around his neck and she kissed him passion-ately, her body rubbing against his.

Shocked, Erin turned, fled back to the car and raced home. She had recognized the woman—Janis, the ten-nis coach. His old girlfriend. Jordan had lied. Janis was definitely still in his life.

Erin felt ridiculously jealous and revolted beyond words. Hadn't he told her he loved her only an hour ago? Did he tell Janis that too? And how many others? Erin was astonished at her own anger. How could she possibly explain his betrayal?

In a fit of pure fury, she slammed the car door.

Fortunately, her father had retired. She didn't want to see anyone, knowing it wouldn't take much for her to break into a surging good cry.

After the shock and anger, came the wrenching hurt. Erin would have liked to pull Jordan's teeth out with a pair of rusty pliers. The relationship had been a horrible mistake. She wished she'd never laid eyes on him, but she'd learned her lesson well.

Stay away from good-looking, charismatic men, she repeated like a mantra as she undressed. *Stay away from charismatic men.*

Chapter Twelve

Erin woke from a troubled dream, thinking she heard her father calling her name. Alert, she sat up and listened. Then she heard his weak call. She threw her legs off the bed, grabbed a terrycloth robe, and hurried down the hall, pushing her tousled hair back from her face.

His bedroom door was closed. She placed her hand on the knob and opened it, entering her father's darkened bedroom. He lay flat on his back. Lucky whined on the floor beside him.

"Erin, girl," he wheezed. His eyes looked glazed and his skin was pale. He grimaced and balled his fist.

Her insides curdled. "What is it, Dad? You're sick?"

"Feel weak as a newborn foal."

Fear gripped Erin's heart. He was short of breath,

and she immediately thought about his high blood pressure. Had he forgotten to take his pills with all the excitement of the past weeks? He had started smoking again on the sly. She snatched the telephone from the bedside table and dialed 911.

In a matter of minutes, the paramedics came and whisked her father off to the local hospital. After throwing on jeans and a sweatshirt, Erin followed in the jeep, her hands shaking on the steering wheel with dread.

The paramedics had already wheeled him into the emergency room by the time she arrived. Erin waited anxiously for word. Her first thought was that he'd had a heart attack. She called Stuart to ask him to watch over things at the ranch until she got back. But he had already left for work. Sarah, too, was out. She made a call to Jordán, telling herself she must be out of her mind.

"God, I'm sorry! I'll be right over, Erin," Jordan said when she told him what had happened.

"Thanks."

"Don't worry. I'll take care of everything. There's not much going on here, anyway," he lied, although his desk was filled with important papers needing his attention. He would come back to his office and stay until midnight, if need be, but he wanted to help Erin.

In the afternoon Erin came back to the ranch. Exhausted, she answered his questions with minimal words.

"Thanks for filling in," she said. "Stu will be along in a couple of hours and I'll go back over to the hospital then."

"I'll take you."

She didn't meet his eyes. "No need. I'll take over now. Thanks again for your help."

"Do you have any idea how long will your father be hospitalized?"

"I don't know yet. They're doing tests. They think it was a mini stroke. Gave it a fancy name. I'm still not sure of anything, but he'll probably be okay if he takes care of himself." She fought back tears. "That'll be something, won't it, trying to get him to do that?"

Her remark twisted Jordan's gut. "I'm really sorry, Erin."

She gave him a fragile smile. "I know you're busy. No need to stick around."

He hated having to leave her alone, wanting to remain there and comfort her. But she looked as though she wanted solitude. "I checked all the horses. They've got plenty of feed and clean water. There's a message on your answering machine in the office, too. The vet, I think."

"Good."

"I'll call you later to see how Mike's doing. Don't hesitate to give me a buzz if you need anything."

He reached out to her but she drew back sharply.

"Thanks again," she said in a brittle voice.

"Erin, what is it?"

Not waiting for him to ask anything more, she turned her back on him and headed toward the house.

He started to follow but she closed the door, leaving him feeling undecided.

Erin took her father home the next day. He fussed when she made him go straight to bed.

"The doctor says you must rest, take your medication and keep your activities to a minimum for a few days. And you can just forget about smoking. It's forbidden fruit from now on." She opened the bedside drawer, took out a package of cigarettes, and crumpled them in her hand. "You were lucky this time, Dad. But if you don't watch it and take care of yourself, it could be far worse next time."

"You sound like my mother," he grunted.

His left hand was weak and his left eye dropped but otherwise he seemed unaffected. Erin still wasn't ready to relax over the whole incident.

"And you'll be going to physical therapy for a while," she said.

"I get all the physical activity I need right here," he retorted.

She puffed up like a mother hen. "You'll do what the doctor says, Dad. We've got to get you back in shape."

Later, when she returned from the stables to check on him, Erin was taken aback when she found a woman sitting beside his bed.

Deep in conversation, her father looked up. "You remember Edith Landon, Erin, don't you?"

Erin smiled. The woman, a widow, had danced with him several times at the barn dance, and she'd seen her in church. "Yes. Nice of you to come by."

"I'm one of the ladies of the hospital auxiliary. When I heard Mike had been admitted, why I just had to come by his room and say hello. He told me I simply had to pay him a visit when he got home."

"It's lonely here by myself," he smirked.

"Stop by anytime," Erin said to her. Her father's coloring looked better. "I just wanted to see if Dad needed anything," Erin said. Seeing he was quite well taken care of, she excused herself and left them alone, smiling to herself. Edith Landon apparently had her eye on Mike Fury. Wasn't that what Erin wanted, someone he could care about again?

Jordan vowed he'd telephone Erin one more time. If she didn't answer, he'd march over to the ranch and demand to know why she was avoiding him. After her father's illness, she seemed more than a little cold but he had laid it to her worry over Mike.

She finally picked up the phone and said hello in a dull voice, unlike her usually energetic greeting.

"Erin? I've been trying to reach you since yesterday. How's your father? They wouldn't tell me anything at the hospital."

"He's home now and I've been busy."

Her tone changed, becoming steely, making him wonder just how bad things actually were at the ranch.

"Anything I can help you with?" he asked.

"No, Jordan. I have to run now."

She hung up, leaving him miffed by her dismissal. Just what was she thinking?

That night, he called again. "Erin, are you okay?"

"You've caught me at a busy time."

"That's what you said last time. I'm merely calling to say hi."

"We have nothing to say to each other."

"Wait just a minute. I'm confused. What is this? Did I do something?"

Then she let him have it in scathing tones that

burned his ear—all about what she'd seen when she came back to his place.

He couldn't believe what he was hearing. "No, that's not what happened!"

"Don't play games with me," she sputtered. "I know what I saw. You and your tennis girlfriend in a clinch! How could you even call me, Jordan Archer!"

"Calm down, will you?" He felt panicky. "Erin? Don't hang up."

He heard her heavy sigh and he rushed on, fearing she would. "I didn't invite Janis over and I didn't initiate that kiss, darn it. She threw herself at me. She had this cracked idea I wanted her back. Too many martinis at dinner, I guess."

"Uh-huh."

"I got rid of her right away. She probably followed you out of the complex. Let me come over, Erin. We've got to talk about this."

"We are talking, and I don't want to see you."

"Honest to God, this is all a big mistake. I'm coming over with or without your permission, and don't run off somewhere, hear?"

He hung up and headed for his car.

Erin was already on the porch waiting, tapping her foot impatiently, and looking none too pleased to see him. But he thought he detected a hint of a smile at the corners of her mouth. He let his breath out slowly. If he said the wrong thing it would be worse than ever. He looked at her warily. At least she was willing to let him speak his piece. Maybe things were going better than he'd hoped. Still, he didn't like the reserve in her manner, the stiff thrust of her shoulders when he walked up on the porch.

He wanted to take her in his arms and reassure her that she was the only one he cared about. But he figured he'd better hold off, from the tight-lipped, reserved message he was getting. At least she wasn't screaming. He tried to stay calm, but he felt as though he was walking on eggshells.

"Want a coke?" she asked very formally.

"Coke's fine."

She took him inside the house to the kitchen. "Take a chair there at the table."

He swung a leg over the seat and sat, willing his nerves to stay cool. She took a bottle out of the fridge and handed it to him. He opened it and took a hefty swig.

"Can we take a walk?" he asked.

"If you want. The orange grove all right?"

"The grove's great." Anything's great, just as long as they were communicating. He was still shocked that she'd seen Janis at his condo at that precise time. Bad luck was dogging his pursuit of this woman.

"I'll go check on my dad first," she said.

Jordan nodded and took another swallow. She returned and they left the kitchen. He tried to take her hand but she rebuffed him. They strolled down between rows of trees, saying little, until they came to a wooden bench by a small storage shack. He reached out and took her hand again. This time she didn't draw away. He turned it over and examined the small callous where a horse's reins had rubbed. To him her hand was the daintiest, most feminine hand he'd ever seen. He made a pattern on her palm with his index finger.

"Erin, this has all been a terrible misunderstanding

and I want to explain about what you thought you saw."

"What I thought I saw? Ha!" She removed her hand.

He hurried on. "Honestly, it's like I told you. I didn't know Janis was coming over. How could I have known? I'd invited you over, right?"

Erin didn't argue. Her large, expressive eyes glanced away.

"Sure, she wanted us to get back together. I told her no way. The next thing I knew she was kissing me. I had to pull her off and call her a cab. I didn't trust her to drive home, she'd had so many."

Erin brought her full attention back to him and crossed one knee over the other, twining her legs. "Is there anything else you have to tell me?"

"Yes, as a matter of fact, there is."

Her quiet demeanor made him uneasy. "I'm not some kind of Lothario. I care deeply for you and only for you."

She thought a long time. Waiting, his nerves felt jumbled, but he wasn't about to give up. Then she put her hand over his. It took him by surprise. "I do believe you, Jordan. And I admit I was terribly hurt, and jealous too, by what I saw."

His heart stopped pounding like a bass drum. He could smell the fragrant orange blossoms again, feel himself breathe normally. The breeze lifted her hair beguilingly. He curled a finger around a lock, kissed it, then reached up to give her a feather-light kiss. Her lips were warm. He deepened the kiss, then she leaned back and looked at him, wide-eyed.

He slipped an arm around her shoulders and pulled her to him. She didn't resist. "You'll never know how happy I am," he said, bending to kiss her throat. Her fingers strayed to his hair and she let them run lightly through the dark strands, making his skin tingle with awareness. Beneath his shirt his heart swelled with longing.

She tilted her face up to his. He pulled her onto his lap. When his mouth covered hers, the kiss was hungry and searching.

On the night of the rally, three days before the extension of the lease was up, Erin finished dressing. She wore a Levi skirt and western blouse. Deep into her gloomy reverie about losing the ranch, doubts about Jordan came back to nibble at the corners of her heart. No matter what she and her father might do, the board of trustees would never change their minds. A few minutes later, when Erin came out of the house and saw several hundred people gathered for the rally, she was stunned. She had never in her wildest dreams expected such a turnout. Support had literally come out of the woodwork. They approached her in waves, some somber-faced, while others looked hopeful. One after another, they patted her on the back and spoke encouraging words. Tears welled in her eyes but she fought them. This was no time to get sentimental. Cheered by the support, she stopped doubting herself and embraced the first person who walked up. It was Stuart.

"I'm sort of frightened," she told him. "Overwhelmed might be a better word. But I'm so happy to see all these people. It's more than I ever expected."

"Come on," he said. "Let's get started. I built the biggest bonfire you've ever seen right in front of the paddock. People are dancing around it like a May Day festival."

Erin looked at the flickering orange fire. The wood crackled and spit, sending sparks into the night sky. The scene revived her spirits.

Stuart grasped her waist and helped her up onto the buckboard they were using as a stage. He stood beside her. Her father was already there, and he looked pleased, if a tad fidgety as he held out his hands and asked for quiet, calling the gathering to order.

"You all know why we're here," he boomed into the microphone. "We face the threat of losing our lease and having to shut down our operations."

The crowd booed, and when they quieted, a resident owl hooted from the top of the barn, causing everyone to laugh.

Mike went on in a steady voice. "Good people, to-night we're going to storm the great wall and show the college trustees we're a united front." His remarks drew cheers. "We're pleased to have a big crowd, so we'll keep our remarks short. We also have the press here." Everyone clapped. "Now Erin, my daughter, wants to say a few words."

Erin stepped forward. "We are here tonight because we need the college board to look at their social responsibility and not at their balance sheet. This issue cries out for community support, and thanks to you all, we have it," she said with conviction. "Through the years so many of you have had a hand in making our ranch a success. We have spent many wonderful hours in your company, and we can only give you our deepest expressions of gratitude for supporting us." She smiled warmly. "Despite our best efforts, time is running out. Whatever happens next, your presence here tonight means so much to us. Please accept our heartfelt thanks."

The loyalists cheered like sports fans. People stepped up and told the gathering how much the ranch meant to them. Sarah took the microphone but began crying and had to give it back to Erin. Stuart spoke about the foal, and how he planned to give it to the Furys.

"That's how it is at the Fury ranch," he said with emotion. "The children need the opportunity to watch Champ grow into a fine riding horse."

A man got up and said how much riding a horse meant to his disabled daughter. "She can't walk but she can have the pleasure of handling a horse, thanks to the Furys," he said, choking up. "I'm not going to let the college fat-cats take that away from her."

The meeting quickly turned into a heart-warming, sharing event. Tears flowed and frustrations mounted.

Stepping forward, Erin shouted, "Let's march to the board of trustees meeting in mass and demand to be heard."

Everyone cheered. Uniformed Boy Scouts and Girl Scouts were there, along with their parents. College students showed up. Members from the Sierra Club attended, along with another animal rights group and an environmental group. Several off-duty sheriff deputies lent their services so that no crowd control problems might arise.

Jordan arrived late. He stood back in the shadows watching Erin. He couldn't help but be proud of the way she stood on the buckboard talking to each and every one of the people gathered there. The woman ought to go into politics, he thought with an inner smile. Earthy and charming, she looked radiantly up-beat. He could see how she grew on people. Now, he simply had to show his solidarity to the Furys' cause. Nothing else would do.

You're a wide-eyed wonder, Erin Fury.

Jordan had seen her come out of the house. Her face looked troubled for only a brief moment. He respected her fortitude and enthusiasm for her cause, even her stubbornness. Nor had he missed the adoration on Stu-art Wilson's face when she hugged him. It caused Jor-dan's jealousy to mount. Those two had too much in common, darn it. Well, Jordan had things in common with her too, like their passion for each other. He wanted to protect her—her innocence, her honesty. He never wanted her to look like a defeated woman.

With his eye on Erin, Jordan came forward and mounted the wagon. Having put away his suit and tie and donned blue jeans and boots, he straightened and held up his hands. Scattered boos rippled through the crowd when he introduced himself.

"I know what you're fighting for," he said. "It's a great cause."

Wary, only a few people clapped, mostly the college students.

He went on.

"The Furys have taught the children that nothing is impossible if you want it badly enough. I want you to know that I'm with you on this, no matter what the cost to me personally. Your children's' well-being should always come first. The Furys deserve the best for their years of dedication."

The clapping increased.

After Jordan finished telling them about his change of heart, everyone burst into a round of applause. Erin stood there a moment, dumbfounded. She felt dizzy, and she spoke to him in a quavering voice, nearly overcome by a tumult of emotions. "They'll fire you," she whispered softly.

His eyes glowed. "Stop worrying. I had to have my say."

Erin looked at him in wonder. She still couldn't quite understand. Yet Jordan really did seem happy about what he'd said. "Jordan . . ."

"It's done—over."

"I thought you loved your job? Speaking at this rally has put your career in jeopardy."

"Erin, I accepted that position like some sort of a trophy—something I thought I had to have. But there have always been things I wanted more."

"But . . ."

"Shush. We'll talk about it later."

He took her in his arms and kissed her, there in front of everyone. The crowd cheered, and he released her immediately, his face flushed for once.

Even still, Erin felt a stab of guilt. It it wasn't for her he'd still be behind that fancy desk, happily going about his work. Now she wasn't so sure.

His eyes flashed with the kind of spirit she had never seen. "We'll win yet! Mark my words. Now, aren't we all supposed to march over to the board meeting?"

"How did you find out?"

"And why didn't you tell me, by the way? I ran into Sarah at a sandwich shop. She told me."

Erin let a small glint of impatience cross her face.

"That was supposed to be a secret. I didn't want you involved."

"Me, involved? I've been entangled in all this from the beginning, remember?"

"Yes, but . . ."

"Let's get on with it."

Everyone took time to light white candles. Then, like crusaders from another era, they silently swept down the road and across the campus to the administration offices. Mike road his horse, leading the procession.

As many people as possible swelled into the building. Herrington, seated in his big leather chair, stood up, frowning in disbelief as they continued to squeeze in. The trustees looked to be in a snit, squirming and craning their necks.

"What a bunch of wonks!" Erin muttered to herself.

Herrington cleared his throat indignantly, eyeing Jordan. "What is the meaning of this? You are not on the agenda."

Jordan stepped to the microphone. "Herrington, the Furys are now on your cotton-picking agenda."

The chairman's face blanched.

Moral pigmy, Erin thought, proud of the way Jordan glared him down.

Herrington chafed. "Why are you here? We have an important meeting going on with one of the county officials."

"I've learned many lessons in my life," Jordan said, loud enough for everyone in the room to hear him. "Somehow I forgot a good number of them along the way. But Erin Fury and her father made me recall that helping others to have fulfilling days was life-affirming in itself. Now they're here tonight to have their say, along with a lot of other people who believe they are in the right and you are in the wrong."

Jordan's eyes grew hard and his voice rose, fairly echoing in the chamber. "The Furys must be allowed to keep the ranch for at least another year. You're not in that big of a hurry. The higher enrollments are only projected. There's that piece of land the college has an option on. Build on that property first. It's only a half mile away. The Furys are rendering a necessary service to the community. Let them continue their excellent work." He looked around at all the faces. "These people have come here tonight in support of the Furys. Hear their stories. If you turn them down again, we'll be back tomorrow to picket the college, and the next day and the next, until you listen to reason."

The trustees grumbled among each other, while the county official scowled at Herrington.

"Many of your own students are here with us," Jordan went on. "By volunteering, they have learned to assess themselves by a higher standard. They've come to realize that their worth isn't determined by having designer clothes and fast cars, but by the contributions they make to their world. We're proud of them."

The meeting turned into chaos. Everyone was talking at once. The newspaperman snapped pictures for the morning paper. The trustees looked chagrined, knowing that after tonight they would look bad. Several of the students threatened to enroll elsewhere next semester.

In his attempt to put a cap on the damage, Herrington hastily huddled with the trustees and they decided to grant the Furys another year. Everyone in the audience cheered. It was like being at a football game in which the quarterback had just run the ball through the goal posts, scoring the victory.

After it was over, Herrington took Jordan aside. "You know what this means?" he said, his eyes unwavering.

"You'll have my resignation on your desk tomorrow morning."

"A proper decision!"

Jordan turned away and smiled, not about to let his getting the sack mar the Furys' triumph. It pleased him to see Erin greet the ruling with joy and relief. She flew into his arms and hugged his neck.

"I can't believe it! They actually caved in," she cried. Then she turned and hugged her father.

"Hon, we did it!" Mike said in his excitement. He patted Jordan on the back.

Edith stood beside him. "You need some fresh air, Mike, dear," she said, and led him outside.

Sarah and Stuart hugged Erin too, along with other people in the stuffy room. Jordan stood back, knowing Erin was close to tears.

When they came out of the building, he looked up. The moon wore a fuzzy halo. He took a sharp breath. Now that everything had changed, he needed time to internalize it. He slipped his arm around her waist and they let the procession back to the ranch. Erin looked so joyful.

Jordan had made the ultimate choice. He helped the Furys stay on the ranch but lost his prestigious job. Yet he knew Erin Fury would always come first.

Chapter Thirteen

Erin scanned the front page of the newspaper the next morning. When she saw Jordan's picture she almost choked. "College President Fired!"

One professor was quoted as saying, "We will miss Dr. Archer's cool head, steady hand, and sharp mind."

The bad news was just what she had feared. The trustees had taken their revenge. Someone had to pay and that someone was Jordan Archer. The battle was won but the cost had been dear to him. The sweet taste of victory turned to vinegar on her tongue. What could she do now? Then it hit her. She'd tell the fuzzy-headed trustees the Furys would move if they'd relent and give Jordan back his job. She ran outside to the barn to show the article to her father and tell him what they must do. Reluctantly he agreed.

198

Erin was heading for her Jeep Cherokee when she saw Jordan coming up the drive in a flurry of dust. He hopped out of the car. She came forward to greet him, concerned about what happened, and told him what she intended to do.

"You shouldn't lose your job because of us," she said.

"I absolutely forbid your doing any such thing," he told her in no uncertain terms.

Erin was stung by his sharp words. "But Jordan, this wouldn't have happened if you hadn't stood up for us."

He took her in his arms and assured her he hated the job and planned to quit at the end of the school year anyway.

"All I ever wanted to do was teach environmental studies and write a book or two."

"You're serious?"

"I couldn't be more so. You woke me up, darling. There are more important things than driving a BMW and wearing an expensive suit. And I certainly won't miss those boring board meetings. You don't know how often I almost fell asleep while Herrington blabbered on. In truth I lacked enthusiasm for that job after the first few weeks."

"But losing it because of us . . ."

"No more recriminations. I'm energized about starting over."

She smiled. "I love you."

He kissed her. "And I worship you."

"I bet you're one humdinger of a teacher."

He looked pleased. "I've got to run now but I'll see you tomorrow."

She let him go, still feeling just awful about his losing his distinguished job, no matter what he might say.

The next day, Erin was a bundle of activity, doing all those things a person puts off when they're under stress. She hurried to the stables and wrestled down a bale of hay by herself, snipped the binding wires, and began spreading the pungent green stuff around.

By six that evening, she felt tired but satisfied. The telephone rang and she dragged herself to the office and picked up the receiver.

"Fury Ranch."

Jordan was on the line. Her heart fluttered, and all the tiredness washed away.

"Erin? I need to see you right away." His voice was soft, no more than a whisper.

"Sure, Jordan."

"Alone."

"The garden?" she said, a smile in her voice.

"Fine. See you in twenty minutes."

She was already waiting, leaning forward in the glider swing, when he drove up and got out. The sight of him stirred her love and she jumped up, fluffing her hair, knowing she must look a sight.

The morning glories climbing on the trellis began closing with the oncoming shadows of evening.

"What is it? Something wrong?" she asked, concerned by the serious look in his eyes.

"Nothing that seeing you won't fix."

He gave her a hug and they sat down in the swing. A muscle in his jaw tightened.

She noticed the razor nick on his chin. "You look so grave."

"I could hardly get through the day without seeing you, hearing your voice." He exhaled, as though he had been holding his breath. "Darling, I can't get along without you."

His strained tone set off an instant alarm in her brain. Had something terrible happened?

He slipped an arm around her shoulders. "You do know that, don't you, Erin?"

"You've just floored me, that's all," she told him honestly. "I don't know how to respond?"

"How could I say it any clearer? I want you to marry me. I love you and cherish you. I adore the ground you walk on."

Thunderstruck, she blurted, "Yes, I'll marry you."

Her throat tightened and she tried to breath normally. Filled with a sudden, intense joy, she grabbed him around the neck and gave him the unbridled kiss she'd wanted to give him ever since they'd met.

They embraced and he kissed her, as happy as a kid on his first date.

He couldn't hold back the grin that spread across his face. "I've been hired to teach at the University of California at Irvine, in the fall."

"Why, that's only fifteen minutes from here!"

His eyes danced. "Well, I'm glad you agreed you'll marry me. Otherwise, I'd have to lock you in a dark closet until you succumbed to my passionate advances." He laughed and drew her onto his lap. "I love your pretty face, your smile, everything about you. I love your quiet confidence, the way you stick out your little finger when you gesture."

She giggled. "Maybe we could find one of those closets, you handsome hunk."

He laughed, then rubbed her cheek with his. A little moan escaped her lips and her finger trailed lightly across his chest. His hand roamed her back. He kissed her with rising hunger and the kiss became more urgent.

"You're everything to me," he murmured.

She cuddled her body into him, content to be in his arms. "I'm so happy," she said softly.

"Me too, darling."

With her compassion and courage, Erin's world had become his. He didn't need power for success. A man must use his heart as well as his head.

Jordan was already in negotiations with Jim O'toole to buy the man's land, and planned to make the Furys full partners. But Jordan had decided not to tell Erin until the deal closed. He wanted to kiss her too much now.

DATE DUE

JUN 2 0 00			
5-28-00			

Charlotte County Library
P.O. Box 788
Charlotte C.H., VA 23923

DEMCO